Coke Kings 4

T.J. Edwards

Lock Down Publications and Ca$h Presents
Coke Kings 4
A Novel by *T.J. Edwards*

T.J. Edwards

Lock Down Publications
Po Box 944
Stockbridge, Ga 30281

Visit our website @
www.lockdownpublications.com

Copyright 2020 T.J. Edwards
Coke Kings 4

All rights reserved. No part of this book may be reproduced in any form or by electronic or mechanical means, including information storage and retrieval systems without permission in writing from the publisher, except by a reviewer who may quote brief passages in review.
First Edition September 2019
Printed in the United States of America

This is a work of fiction. Names, characters, places, and incidents either are products of the author's imagination or are used fictitiously. Any similarity to actual events or locales or persons, living or dead, is entirely coincidental.

Lock Down Publications
Like our page on Facebook: Lock Down Publications @
www.facebook.com/lockdownpublications.ldp
Cover design and layout by: **Dynasty Cover Me**
Book interior design by: **Shawn Walker**
Edited by: **Lashonda Johnson**

Stay Connected with Us!

Text **LOCKDOWN** to 22828 to stay up-to-date with new releases, sneak peaks, contests and more…

Thank you.

T.J. Edwards

Submission Guideline.

Submit the first three chapters of your completed manuscript to ldpsubmissions@gmail.com, subject line: Your book's title. The manuscript must be in a .doc file and sent as an attachment. Document should be in Times New Roman, double spaced and in size 12 font. Also, provide your synopsis and full contact information. If sending multiple submissions, they must each be in a separate email.

Have a story but no way to send it electronically? You can still submit to LDP/Ca$h Presents. Send in the first three chapters, written or typed, of your completed manuscript to:

LDP: Submissions Dept
Po Box 944
Stockbridge, Ga 30281

DO NOT send original manuscript. Must be a duplicate.

Provide your synopsis and a cover letter containing your full contact information.

Thanks for considering LDP and Ca$h Presents.

Dedications

This book is dedicated to my amazingly, beautiful stomp down wife, Mrs. Jelissa Shante Edwards, who knows firsthand what this Ski Mask life is all about.

I've had to feed our family many nights using that to make it happen. But, for you, I had to find another way because you deserve the best, and my place to be is beside you, protecting you at all times.

You're my motivating force that keeps me going. No matter how old you get, you'll always be my baby girl. So, deal with it. I love you forever and always.

Your husband.

R.I.P to my beautiful mother, Deborah L. Edwards

Shout out to Cash and Shawn. I love y'all with all my heart…not only as a C.E.O and C.O.O, but as brother and sister. This is me and my wife's home. You already know that our loyalty is sealed in blood. Mad love to the entire LDP family.

T.J. Edwards

Chapter 1

"How much is it going to take? What is it going to cost us for you to let my woman go, and for you to leave us the fuck alone?" While these were the words coming out of Duke's mouth, he wasn't thinking about anything other than revenge. He simply wanted to get them out of the sticky situation. He would deal with Jason and his Yonkers crew accordingly after that.

Jason rubbed his chin with one hand and held the chainsaw in his other. "Word on the street is that Kammron got some serious M's put up, at least ten. Nigga, we ain't leaving Harlem, angling back to Yonkers, until we got at least five of them jokers. That's the price for your shorty right here, and time is running out. It looks like she's a bleeder." He nodded at Shana with his head.

Shana had blood oozing out of her wound as sweat saturated her face. She breathed heavily and hung tirelessly against her chains.

Duke swallowed and exhaled loudly. "Yo, if I can get you five million, you and yo niggas a leave Harlem for good?"

Jason nodded. "You muthafuckin' right. But I'ma need that shit in cash, in less than twenty-four hours. If you ain't back here with that scratch by then, not only is this bitch finna get the bidness, but some of the homies made a pit stop to Philly, and we just so happened to stumble up on this li'l broad, too." He snapped his fingers and stood back with a mug on his face.

Duke's heart nearly fell out of his chest when he saw the way one of Jason's monsters were handling his daughter, Deanna. The man held her by the back of her neck roughly. Her mouth was taped with silver duct tape, and she was crying. She had handcuffs on her wrists, and shackles on her six-year-old ankles.

Duke tried his best to break away from the chains. "Arrgh, dis ain't got nothin' to do with her. Let my muthafuckin' shorty go," he yelled.

Jason kneeled in front of the crying Deanna. He rubbed her face. "Aw, po' baby, you're so pretty. You don't look nothing like yo' ugly ass daddy, luckily for you." He looked over at Duke and cheesed. "How old are you, baby girl?" He knew she couldn't answer him because her mouth was covered with the tape, but to be an asshole, he placed his ear right on her duct tape. "I'm sorry, Sweetie, I can't hear you. You're going to have to speak up."

Deanna could only cry. She couldn't understand what was going on, and why the men had hurt her mommy, and took her away. Nothing made sense, if this was a game her father was playing, she didn't like it. It was too scary.

Jason stood up, grabbed a handful of Deanna's hair, and mugged Duke. "You got twenty-two hours to come up with my gwop. Find my cash, or find both of these hoes floating in the Harlem River. That's word to Uptown." He broke into laughter and gave the signal to his men so they could snatch up Duke and drop him off in a random place in New York.

***

Henny crawled nakedly across the bed and climbed atop Kammron. She laid her cheek against his and rubbed the side of his face. "Daddy, I'm so turnt up, I can't think straight. My whole body is tingling," she mumbled.

Kammron was high as a kite as well. They had spent the entire day shooting China. He felt like he was on a planet of euphoria. He licked his lips and rubbed his hands down the small of Henny's lower back until he was cuffing her ass. He still couldn't believe how strapped she really was. "Yo, it's like I told you, you fuck with me, you ain't finna have to worry about nothing. It'll be smiles from here on out. That's what a daddy is supposed to do."

Henny dubbed her bald kitty up and down Kammron's stomach, leaving a trail of her essence. "Daddy, I'm so horny. I need you. I'm fiendin'." She slid her hand under her stomach and opened her sex lips, before slipping her middle finger up her box. The sensation coupled with the China was enough to make her shudder.

Kammron opened her ass cheeks and trailed a digit around her tight rosebud. He dipped his middle finger into her hole and pulled it back out. "I wanna fuck this young ass, Henny. Daddy wanna hit this back door. You wanna give me some of that?" He squeezed her ass again, his piece began to telescope against her body.

Henny felt it and moved up on his frame. She trapped the head of his piece between her sex lips, rotating her hips against his lap. Her eyes closed and rolled into the back of her head. "Mmm-mmm-mmm, Daddy! Unnhh-unnhhh-yes, Daddy!" Her coochie got wetter and wetter in a matter of seconds as she grinded against him.

Kammron simply held her ass and laid back. What she was doing felt good. His fingers crept into her crevice. He played with her juices and sucked on her neck.

"Uhhhh, Daddy!" More jumping, and grinding. "Fuck me, please, please, Daddy. I'm begging you." Her kitty was on fire.

She grabbed a hold of Kammron's dick, and started to stuff him into her box, as soon as his head peeked through her entrance, she slammed down on him and started riding him as her breasts slapped up and down. "Unnhhh-unnhhh-unnhhh,

11

Daddy! Daddy-ooo-ooo, fuck yes!" She held the top of the headboard for leverage and worked him.

Kammron leaned up and sucked one erect nipple, then the next. His tongue ran circles around each one. Then he was kissing in between the globes and licking up her sweat. Her pussy felt like a hot glove wrapped around his pipe. She was so wet it was running out of her and making a puddle under both of their asses.

"Yeah, baby, ride Daddy! Ride Daddy, ride Daddy—ride Daddy! Shit—ride me!" He gripped her cheeks and proceeded to slam her forward, making sure she was taking his entire length.

"Here I—uhhhh, here I—cum, Daddy! Fuck—uhhhh," she screamed, and began working him as hard and as fast as she could. Then she was shaking, and her cat began to spit love juices all over him.

Kammron flipped her on her stomach and slightly parted her thighs. He smacked her ass and watched her chubby cheeks jiggle. He opened her booty wide and ran his tongue in circles around her rosebud. When he got it nice and dripping, he grabbed the K-Y from the dresser and stroked his piece with it, getting it nice and lubed. Then he slowly worked his dick into Henny's ass.

She grabbed ahold of the sheets and balled it into her small hand. "Unnhhh, daddy." Her hand snuck between her thick thighs to manipulate her clit. She pinched and rolled her middle finger around it.

After Kammron pulled her up to all fours, he eased into her back door slowly and stroked her lovely at first. Then sped up the pace and proceeded to fuck her like a Porn star, digging deep into her backdoor.

Henny grinned, and it didn't take long before she was loving what he was doing to her. As long as she kept her fingers on her clit, the China allowed all her sexual senses to be heightened times a hundred. "Fuck me, daddy! Fuck me-fuck me, yes! Unnhhh, daddy, yes-yes! I'm yours—I'm yours," she moaned. Kammron watched his pipe run in and out of her. It drove him crazy. He slapped her ass hard. It jiggled and motivated him to go savage mode on her. "Uh-uh-uh-uh, uhhhh shit, Henny! Baby girl, daddy—uhhhh!" He began cumming hard, slamming into her as deep as he could go. Then he was falling on top of her.

****

Duke felt like he couldn't breathe. He was running as fast as he could and had been ever since Jason's men dropped him off in Ruckers Park. When he made it onto Kammron's street, he struggled to keep up the same pace. He made it to his stoop before he stopped to take a breather. His lungs felt as if they were inflamed. He swallowed his spit and could taste the blood mixed with mucus. He gathered himself and rushed up the steps, beating on the door.

Kammron sat upright in bed. He grabbed a .40 Caliber from under his pillow, looked over and saw Henny sitting on the love seat just sliding the syringe into her vein. She pushed down on the feeder as her eyes rolled into the back of her head. Kammron jumped up and rushed into the hallway.

He ran to the front of the house naked, and placed his back to the door. "Who the fuck is that beating on my door?"

Duke continued to try and catch his breath. "It's me, Kammron. Open the fuckin' door, B." Duke looked over his shoulder.

Three Expeditions pulled to the curb with Kammron's security inside of them. They were ready to annihilate Duke because, at first, they couldn't identify him. But when they made him out, they pulled away from the curb and continued to make their rounds in the neighborhood.

"Duke, why the fuck are you beating on the door like you're crazy? Have you lost your fuckin' mind?" Kammron snapped. He peeked out of the window and made sure it was actually him.

Duke held his head down. "Open the door, Kammron. I need your help. Please man, this shit is serious bidness."

Kammron took a step back and opened the door. He allowed Duke to step into the living room. Duke began to pace back and forth right away. Kammron locked the door back and turned around to face Duke. "What the fuck happened to your face, Duke?"

"Dem Yonkers niggas, B. Kid, they fucked me up. They got Shana and my daughter, Deanna, man." Duke felt like he was minutes away from becoming hysterical. He really didn't know what to do.

Kammron mugged him. "How the fuck they get them?"

Duke lowered his head. "They caught me and Shana slipping, coming out of the Boys and Girls club. And apparently, they snatched up my daughter from Philly. I ain't asked how they wound up getting a hold of her because I fear the worst, but one thing is for sure, you gotta help me get 'em back." Duke mugged him when he stopped and noticed Kammron was actually naked.

Kammron sighed and sat on the arm of the couch. "How the fuck you expect me to help you? I don't know where he is holding them." Kammron got up and headed to his bedroom. He picked his boxers up off the floor and slipped them on. Henny was on the love seat nodding in and out. Every so often, she would scratch herself.

"I'm finna get me a whole stable of young hoes. I'm finna draft these bitches from high school into the pros," he said out loud to nobody. When he made it back into the hallway, Duke was just going into the room where Kammron usually kept the money that was dropped off to him. "Say, nigga, where the fuck are you going?" Kammron yelled.

Duke rushed into the room. "Jason said he needs five million, Kammron. Come on, man, I know we got it. I need that money so I can save my girls, man." Duke's eyes were watery.

He could only imagine what Jason and his crew had in store for Deanna and Shana if he couldn't come up with the money. Duke opened the closet door and removed the wall inside of it. He knew it was where Kammron kept some of his safes that were usually stacked with cash. He thought he should've been able to come up with at least two million and some change. He had close to one million at his own home in a safe. He figured he would put what he had along with what he came up with from Kammron and get as close to five million as possible.

"Come on, Kammron, help me pull these safes out of here."

Kammron mugged him again. "Bruh, what the fuck is you talking about? I ain't said I was finna allow my money to get caught up in the middle of whatever is going on. That shit ain't got nothin' to do wit' me. Shana is yo' responsibility now, not the kid's. Come on, get the fuck out of here." Kammron snapped his fingers and tried to lead Duke toward the hallway by his arm.

Duke yanked his arm away from Kammron. "Nigga, I ain't going nowhere until you give me this money. At the very

15

least, do it for Deanna. She ain't got nothin' to do with none of this bullshit. She's just a kid."

Kammron sucked his teeth. "Duke, you been out here getting money just like me. Nigga, go holla at your stash. I ain't coming off my shit. Far as I'm concerned, this ain't nothing but the spoils of war. The God doesn't negotiate with terrorists. Come on, get out of my shit."

Duke remained with his head down. His chest raised and fell in anger. He couldn't believe how selfish Kammron was being. At that moment, he wanted to take his life. He slowly trailed his eyes up until they were locked on the .40 Caliber that Kammron held.

"A'ight, B, that's how you gon' play shit? Cool then." He made it seem as if he was simply going to walk past him, but as soon as he was close enough, he tackled him into the wall and slammed his hand against the edge of the doorway, causing Kammron to drop the .40. It slid into the hallway, just in front of the door. They rustled and tussled. They wound up on the floor wrestling, with Duke on top.

"I need that money, Kammron. Why the fuck are you taking me through all of this? We are supposed to be brothers."

Kammron pumped his hips to toss Duke off him. He sat up and head-butted Duke. Duke flew backward. Kammron slid across the floor on his stomach. He was just about to grab ahold of the gun when Bonkers slammed his Timb on it. Kammron looked up and saw Bonkers with his arm around Henny's neck and a Glock aimed at him. The hallway was cluttered with masked men holding guns and machetes.

Bonkers curled his upper lip. "Am I my brother's keeper, Kammron?"

Chapter 2

Kammron looked up at Bonkers with bucked eyes. He swore he was seeing a ghost. He rushed to the gun that was under Bonkers' Timb, ignoring the fact that Bonkers had a Glock aimed at him. Kammron managed to get the gun from under it. He rolled to his left and cocked the .40 Caliber. He jumped up and aimed his gun at Bonkers. "Fuck you pointing ya gun at me for, Bonkers?"

Bonkers lowered his eyes and laughed under his breath. "Nigga, I done got the full report on how shit been going down ever since I been out of commission, and I gotta say, I don't like what I been hearing, Kammron." Henny struggled against him. He tightened his grip on her neck. "Bitch, stop moving before I make sho you ain't able to no more."

"I don't know who been dropping dirt on my name, nigga, but I'm the only mafucka that been holding you down one hundred percent. Yo shorty and yo bitch been eating real good because of Killa." Kammron mugged him and sized up the army of face painted Jamaicans behind Bonkers. They had the hallway completely cluttered. He was outnumbered and outgunned.

Bonkers shook his head. "N'all, nigga, that's not what was told to me. You see, my update was that from the moment I went down, you got to fuckin' my bitch and playing house. I found out you got a baby by her and all of that, so excuse me for not coming to holler at you on some lovey dovey shit. Duke, you rolling wit dis nigga, too?"

Duke Da God held his jaw. His lips were split from fighting wit' Kammron and he felt like killing him, but he was no pussy. He would handle Kammron on his own terms. That was the law of Harlem. Killas kill killas, not play pussy and seek help. "Yo, we been at odds a li'l bit, but word to the

17

borough, Son been holding you down and handling all of ya financials. He got a whole safe that's stacked for you only. He been taking care of ya seed from his own scratch."

"Heard he got a son by Yasmin, and all of that. What's good with that, Duke? Nall, Kammron, what's good wit you having a seed by my shorty?" Bonkers felt his temper rising from the mere thought of Yasmin having Kammron's son.

"Dat shit ain't no guarantee that li'l homey is mine. We fucked a few times that you knew about before you went down, Bonkers. You and I already had this fight. Why are we going through this shit again?" Kammron had heard that after a person was laid up in a coma for weeks on end, one of the things they were deprived of was their memory. He wanted to play this angle on Bonkers.

Bonkers tightened his grip on the gun. "Nigga, I don't remember having this fight wit you, and it's because of you that Yasmin ain't functioning right. She won't even talk to me about none of this without breaking down in tears. You need to tell me what happened between you two because Shana said y'all was a whole ass couple while I was fucked up."

"Yo, that's what we're doing now? We about to listen to a bunch of bitches?" Kammron snapped. "Nigga, I been ya right hand ever since we was yay high. We peed in the same bed and flipped on dirty mattresses as kids. You my mafuckin' day one. Fuck them bitches. Word to God." Kammron made the play of lowering his gun. "I love you too much to get into a gunfight over pussy, so if you gon' kill me, then gon' 'head and do it. Just know I would never cross you."

Duke looked over his shoulder at the closet that Kammron had the four safes filled with cash inside. There had to be at least five million in there, he figured. If Bonkers killed Kammron, it was a guarantee that he would lose Shana and Deanna. He couldn't allow for that to happen. He cleared his throat. "We da set, Bonkers. My nigga, Kammron, don't love nobody like he love you. If you kill him, you gotta kill me, too, because I bare witness that he has been holding you down. He has been at the hospital more than anybody else, that's including Yasmin. If that ain't love, then what is?"

"Don't tell his crazy ass shit, Duke. The nigga wanna kill his most loyal ally, then let him do it. Before you do, though, you need to know that Jimmy got us in some serious bullshit with them Vega boys out of Brooklyn by way of Havana. Them niggas playing for keeps. They got a million dollars a piece on both Jimmy and my head. Now that you're out of that coma, you best believe that it's about to be a million dollar bounty on your shit now, too. You pose even more of a threat because once Jimmy is killed, then the trenches see you as taking over his seat. The slums already know that you and I are basically the same mafucka. They've been knowing that ever since we were dirty ass kids wit' million dollar dreams. Speaking of which." Kammron tucked the gun into the small of his back. He opened the closet door and pulled out two duffel bags of cash that he had yet to stuff into one of his many safes. He dropped them on the floor in front of Bonkers. "That's one million right there. Five stuffed in each bag, and it's yours. Tell me that ain't love."

Henny tried once again to break free of Bonkers' hold. "Let me go," she screamed.

"Bitch, shut up," Kammron snapped.

Henny stood still. She bucked her eyes at Kammron and grew confused.

Bonkers pushed her by the back of the head. She flew into Duke Da God. He caught her. Bonkers knelt with his eyes pinned on Kammron. He unzipped one of the duffel bags and pulled out a ten thousand dollar stack of cash. He thumbed through it. "Well, I'll be damned. Nigga, you seeing cash like this now?"

Kammron nodded. "WE seeing cash like this."

"That's what I'm saying, Bonkers. You and Kammron are the heart and soul of Harlem. You niggas can't be fighting. Right now, the borough needs both of you the most." Duke placed his hand on Kammron's shoulder.

Bonkers zipped up the duffel bag and stood up. "When I walked up, you two was in here fighting, for what?"

"A few niggas from Yonkers invaded Harlem, and they managed to snatch up Shana, and my daughter, Deanna." Duke felt a lump form in his throat.

"I can't do this shit properly without you, Bonkers. I've been trying. That nigga, Jimmy, been too busy focused on the Queens borough, and Jamaica. All the weight has been on my shoulders, and I needed your assistance." Kammron promised himself that when the time was right, not only was he going to kill Bonkers for pulling the .40 cal on him, but he was also going to kill Jimmy and Shana as well. His mind was made up.

"Wait a minute. Why are you more worried about Shana than Kammron?" Bonkers tucked his gun and held both bags in his hands.

"Dats his bitch now. It's been a lot of crazy developments, shit that you'll be brought up to speed on. But for now, we need to figure out what we're going to do about them Vega boys and them niggas from Yonkers. The borough is under the gun."

Bonkers felt a dizzy spell come over him. He fell against the wall and grit his teeth. He kept a stronghold on the handles of the bags. "Yo, I gotta get myself together before I go at anybody. You niggas gotta carry on just like I'm still in that coma until I find out what's going on all across the board. I feel like both of you niggas need to be vetted before I get involved wit either one of you niggas again." He closed his eyes briefly and opened them back. "I need to touch base with Jimmy and Yasmin. When I do that, Kammron, I'll be in touch. Until then, neither one of you niggaz try to contact me. When it's time, I'll contact you." He handed the bags to one of the Jamaican assassins and headed into the hallway.

"It's a few dead bodies outside, yo security I take it. You might wanna clean that shit up and tighten up whatever you supposed to be running, Kammron. This ain't a good look on you." With those words, Bonkers left the trio of Kammron, Duke Da God, and Henny standing inside of the room with startled expressions on their faces.

***

"Come on, Kammron, what I just did was worth every bit of that two million you got in those bags. I know you ain't fuckin' wit Shana like that, but consider this a blessing for Deanna." Duke Da God, was about to open the passenger's door.

Kammron was highly irritated. He couldn't believe that in one night he was set to blow four million dollars. He had one left to his name. He felt like a bum. How the fuck could he be the king of Harlem with only a lousy ass million dollars? He couldn't be.

"Say Son, I know you got ya baby girl in there and all of that, but I'm letting you know right now that I'm getting my money back. I'm not playin', Duke, yo ass is two million dollars in the red."

Duke nodded. "We understand each other." He hopped out of the Porsche and ran along the alley with both bags in his hands. By the time he got across St. Nicholas, he was breathing heavy and had sweat coming down the side of his face. He made it to the apartment building and ran inside. He took the stairs two at a time until he got to the third floor. He ran down the pissy hallway and dropped the bags in front of the door. He beat on it like he was the police, and waited for a few seconds before beating on it again. Now the sweat was really dripping from his face. He waited, and tried the knob. To his surprise, the door opened. He pushed it inward. Two big rats ran out of the entrance, screeching loudly.

"Yo, Jason, I got yo scratch man. I got every penny, son." He stepped into the apartment with his stomach doing somersaults. The apartment was dark and smelled like spoiled meat and feces. Duke wondered why Jason would have him meet him there instead of the basement where they were before. "Jason, P, fuck you niggaz at man?" He felt along the wall for the light switch. He knocked five cockroaches off of the wall before he found it. He flipped it on and waited for his eyes to adjust to the brightness. As soon as they did, he ventured further inside of the apartment.

"Jason, come on, man. Where the fuck is my daughter? Jason," Duke yelled as he kept walking. He was about to stroll past the kitchen when he caught a glimpse of something out of the corner of his eyes. He turned to see what it was and fell to his knees. "Nooooooo."

Shana's head had been severed from her body. They'd placed it on a dinner plate and the head had tipped over. Blood dripped off of the table and onto the kitchen floor. The rest of her body was propped up in a chair that was around the table. On the refrigerator, written in blood, were the words: Hostile Takeover.

Duke began to run all around the house looking for Deanna. "If you muthafuckas hurt my baby, I swear to God it's about to be war. When he was sure that he checked the house from top to bottom and was unable to find her, he pulled out his iPhone and called Jason.

Jason picked up on the third ring. "Damn shame what happened to Shana, ain't it? I wonder what yo' li'l micro bitch will look like all cut up and thangs?" He laughed.

"You bitch ass nigga. I got yo' money. Where is my baby?" Duke snapped.

"We don't give a fuck how young they is in Yonkers, kid, word up. Check dis out, the fee is ten million and Kammron gotta surrender Harlem to Yonkers. If not, yo daughter gon' receive the kiss of death, after we party her li'l ass."

Duke imagined a bunch of grown men defiling his baby girl and retched his guts. "Yo, chill, homey. What the fuck you want me to do?" He felt ready to panic.

"I'll be in touch, nigga. For now, fall back and yo daughter will stay alive, and that's only because you got value. The second your value goes away, that's when this li'l bitch will have a tag on her toe." The phone went dead.

Duke stumbled and fell to his knees again. He broke all the way down until his forehead was on the floor. "She doesn't deserve this shit. She doesn't deserve this." He cried his heart out for the next ten minutes. Then he got up and kissed Shana on the forehead, before breaking away from the scene.

T.J. Edwards

Chapter 3

A month later...

"Yo, Killa, it's been a whole ass month and ain't nobody seen Jason or P. I'm starting to get worried about Deanna, man. If one of them niggas touched my baby girl, I'ma lose my mind." Duke chopped his razor blade through the China White heroin and separated it into four thin lines. He put the straw inside of his right nostril, and cleared the entire path of dope. He switched the straw into the left nostril, and did the same thing with it, tooting hard.

Kammron placed the last stack of money into the money machine and waited for it to count it. "Ain't shit I'ma be able to tell you, Duke, that'll make you feel better. You already know how we get down in the set, though. Ain't no fuckin' way we have a hostage for a whole ass month without deading they ass." Kammron watched the digital numbers appear on the money counter. It read twenty one thousand.

"Don't get me thinking crazy, Killa. I already..." Duke's eyes slowly closed. He leaned forward as if he were getting ready to fall off of the couch. He started to snore loudly. The potent heroin taking over him.

Kammron placed the twenty thousand dollars into the Duffel bag that was already stuffed with two hundred and nineteen thousand dollars. He clapped his hands together loudly. "Duke!"

Duke's eyes popped open. "What, what, shit." He lazily reached for the gun that was on his waist and got ready to pull it from his belt. His eyes became heavy again and he nodded back out.

"Nigga, if you don't wake yo goofy ass up, I swear I'm about to break yo jaw. Wake up!" Kammron clapped his hands together again.

Duke jumped up and rubbed his eyes. His mouth was dry and his eyelids felt like they were being pulled down by anvils. "Yo, Killa, why do you keep making all dis mafuckin' noise? You ruining my high."

"Nigga, fuck yo high. This is only two hundred and fifty thousand total. Where is the rest of my money?" Kammron scooted to the edge of the couch and mugged Duke.

"I told you I'ma get it all to you. Fuck you sweating me for?" Duke closed his eyes again and began to nod.

Kammron stood up and pulled out a .45. He cocked it and placed it to Duke's forehead. "Nigga, I know you stressing because Shana got killed and Deanna is missing, but that ain't got shit to do with the word that you gave me. You still down one point five million dollars. I don't play about my cheddah, boy, and you know that. Where is my shit at, Duke?" He pressed the gun more firm to Duke's head ready to blow it off of his shoulders.

Duke opened his eyes and frowned. "Say, kid, get that burner off my forehead. You ain't gon' pull the trigger over no chump change, especially after I saved ya life from Bonkers and all of those crazy ass Jamaicans."

Kammron pulled back the hammer. "Duke, I ain't playin' wit chu. Where the fuck is the rest of my money?"

Duke's face balled into a mask of fury. He slapped the gun off of him. "Man, fuck you, Kammron. You know I got yo' selfish ass as soon as I get it. I've been paying you dollar for dollar. Don't act like you don't see what I got going in these streets."

Kammron was itching to kill Duke. Ever since the tragedy of Shana's murder and the kidnapping of Deanna, Duke had taken to doing heroin all day and night. While he still hustled like a champion, he didn't operate at the same capacity as he had prior to the attacks. Kammron was starting to feel as if he was dead weight. "Look, Duke, you gotta get yo shit together. All that shit that happened is part of the game. We know what we're getting into every time we take a foot out in the streets of New York. This city was built on blood. A mafucka can't survive here unless they are plotting every single second of the day. We got a bunch of blood on our hands, nigga, so you already know how that karma shit work."

"Yeah, but Deanna is just a little girl. She ain't got shit to do with what I got going on in the trenches. Niggas who target kids and women are nothing bitch niggaz. I ain't never got down like that, so why is karma trying to fuck me over?" He leaned his head back to the table and took two more lines.

Kammron shook his head. He didn't give a care about Deanna or Shana. His money was most important over everything. "She should be alright, bruh. In the meantime, we gotta see what's good with Bonkers. That nigga said he'd call once he got shit figured out. It's been a month, and he ain't touched bases with me yet."

"You'd be dead if it wasn't for me, Killa. That fool Bonkers slayed eight of your security men that night. Had I not vouched for you, he would've killed you, too. I am sure of that. A mafucka got you out of that jam and this is how you treat me. Damn, you cold." Duke laid his head back on the couch and nodded back out.

"Man, fuck Bonkers. Don't bring up what you saved me from again. You already ran that shit into the mud. We even, you hear me? You gon' pay me the rest of my money and we gon' move forward from there. Can you dig that?"

Duke yawned and nodded. "Yeah, Killa. Nigga, I hear you."

Henny came into the den with a red slim robe tied around her frame. She stepped up to Kammron and kissed him on the cheek. "Daddy, do you remember when you were saying that you wanted to start a stable of young hoes, sign them under the set, having 'em sell pussy and work in a few of your clubs once they get up and running?"

"Yeah, what about it?" Kammron turned to face her, wiping her kiss off of his cheek.

"Well my mother said that my little sister and my little cousin are coming to New York for the summer. Both of them are beautiful and strapped. I don't think they've ever been with anybody before, so you'll be able to break them in. And I'll start snatching up other females, too, so we can get your stable up and running as fast as possible. I just wanna do my part."

"Yeah, it's about time you do because you're starting to get on my mafuckin' nerves, too. I've been thanking 'bout kicking yo' ass to the curb. What's these li'l bitches' names?"

Henny swallowed the lump in her throat. "Monica and Chelsey."

Kammron nodded. "And which one is your sister?"

"Monica."

"She red and thick like you?"

Henny nodded. "Yeah and she's just a tad bit shorter. But she is gorgeous and I know she will listen to me."

"It ain't 'bout her listening to you. That ain't gon' get her nowhere. It's about her falling in line in this stable. If she doesn't, all of her disciplining gon' fall on you, just as much as her. That goes for Chelsey, too. What does she look like?"

"Caramel-skinned, thick, with pretty hazel eyes. She just turned eighteen three days ago. Her father is an Imam in the Muslim community and she's ready to break away from that whole religious household. She said they kept her locked down too much. She wants to be free and live her life."

"Well, like I said, you're starting to wear out yo welcome. It's in yo' best interest to find you some worth real soon." Kammron curled his upper lip.

Henny ran her fingers through her unkempt hair and looked up at him nervously. "Daddy, can I have somethin' to wake me up so I can get on my grind for you?"

"Here we go wit' dis shit. What you need, Henny?" Kammron eyed Duke. He'd fallen forward and onto the floor, snoring loudly. He scratched his neck with a smile on his face.

"Just a little somethin'. You know I never need much." She was anxious. Seeing Duke doubled over caused her to become thirsty for a fix. She wanted to be in the same state that he was in.

Kammron walked to the table that had a kilo of China White on top of it. He spooned up seven grams and placed it inside of a mini Ziploc bag. "Huh, bitch." He tossed it at her.

Henny damn near twisted her ankle to catch it. "Thank you, daddy. And you'll see, I'ma get you a stable together, a stable of jail bait that you're going to be able to make lots of money from." As she said this, she was backing out of the room. She could already imagine what it would feel like to shoot the drug into her system. She started to shiver.

Kammron waved her off. "Go handle yo' bidness, and do what you gotta do. The clock is ticking for yo ass, and the worst case scenario for you is that it expires. You know way too much about my operation, which means that there is only one way that you can be cut loose from the set." Kammron pulled his .45 out of the small of his back and kissed it. "You get my drift?"

All Henny wanted to do was to get high. While she was terrified at what Kammron was getting at, she didn't care in the moment. She continued to back out of the room. "Yeah, Daddy, I get your drift, and trust me, it will never come to that.

Just believe in me, that's all I ask." She stepped into the hallway and closed the door to the den. She took a deep breath and smiled, kissing the sack of dope.

"Yousa dirty ass nigga, Killa." Duke eased back onto the couch. He pulled a Newport from his shirt pocket and sparked it.

"Why am I dirty, Duke?"

"You got that li'l bitch turned all the way out, and now you got her bringing her sister and cousin under your thumb. That's why." Duke laughed. "Yo ass ain't gon' never change."

"Let me explain somethin' to you, Duke. I like young pussy. I fuck wit vets from time to time, but I love bussing down a li'l young bitch. That's just in my nature. Henny, was a force to be reckoned with when I first snatched her up from that car dealership. Now I can't be in the same room with her for too long before she getting on my damn nerves." He plopped down on the couch.

"So, what you gon' do when her sister and cousin get to the point that she is now?" Duke scratched the back of his neck and closed his eyes. "You gon' kick them to the curb, too?"

"You betta know it. Out with the old, and in with the new. There ain't a nigga alive that won't get sick of the same pussy after a while. That's why you gotta keep something fresh ducked off at all times. But fuck that shit. I'm ready to hit that pavement in Harlem. We laid low for a whole month. Now it's time to get back out there."

"You forget that Showbiz Vega got a million dollars on yo head, or what?" Duke opened his eyes to see Kammron's expression.

Kammron sucked his teeth. "Ain't nobody faded Jimmy yet. He be in the trenches every single day and ain't nobody did shit to him. What makes you think that they gon' try and do somethin' to the king of Harlem? Huh?"

"Because Jimmy got a million dollars' worth of security around him at all times. He got Jamaicans and them Queens niggas he done conquered. It's hard for anybody to get next to him."

"And I'm feeding a thousand niggas under me. Mafuckas owe me their loyalty and devotion. Harlem doesn't eat unless Kammron makes that shit happen. Ain't nobody about to let shit happen to me. Besides all of that, I'ma shoot this fully automatic by myself, like I'm shooting a technical foul in basketball. I'm my own mafuckin' shooter. It's time to get to business. The first order is to tear some shit apart all up and down St. Nicholas Avenue, where them Yonkers niggaz rotate. I'm about to set shit in motion. After that, I need to penetrate Bonkers' circle again. We gotta find out if he's fuckin' wit Jimmy the long way, or if he is doing his own thing. Henny say she saw both him and Yasmin on Facebook for Valentine's Day so I guess he still fuckin' wit her, goofy ass nigga. I never could climb aboard the train of sucka for love. I leave that shit to you niggas."

Duke pursed his lips. He felt disrespected. He wanted to check Kammron, but instead of doing so, he kept his comments to himself. "So what do you wanna do first? You on some front lines type shit, or am I handling my business with a team of animals from the borough?"

"When it comes to tracking down those Yonkers niggaz, you on yo own, but I'ma make sure that you have a team around you. I'ma see what's good with Bonkers through a few channels, and then we gon' move on him, too. That punk Jimmy in jeopardy as well. I ain't buying this whole he's 'untouchable' shit. I'ma touch that nigga when the time is right." Kammron stood back up and grabbed the duffel bag of cash. "Duke, get yo ass up and get on the move. The longer you sit here and stew in your misery, the stronger them Yonkers niggas get, and the worst the odds are for Deanna."

Duke nodded. "When you're right, you're right, Killa." He stubbed out his cigarette and stood up on shaky knees. "Let's do this, Dunn."

***

That night, Kammron woke up to a shotgun held against his cheek. His eyes were bucked wide open. He thought about sliding his hand under the pillow to grab his trusted .45, but then decided against it. The culprit had the ups on him. He could smell the steel of the shotgun. He was stuck.

"Motherfucker, if you move, you're a dead man. I swear it. Your rap sheet is as long as Seventh Avenue. If I kill you, the media will make me look like a got damn hero." He pressed the shotgun harder into his cheek, nearly tearing the flesh there. "You're under arrest."

"Yeah, aiight, just get that joint off of my cheek."

Chapter 4

Federal Agent Bishop was Jewish, he was five feet six inches tall, with pale skin and green eyes. He had curly hair around the sides of his head, and a big bald spot smack dead in the middle. He stepped into the interrogation room with Kammron's criminal file in his hand. He pulled the metal chair across the floor, causing it to scratch at the concrete underneath it loudly. He slammed the paperwork down and took a seat across from Kammron.

Kammron was jarred awake, and now feeling the effects of what being away from his heroin for ten hours felt like. His stomach was in knots. He kept retching inside of his mouth, and forced to swallow it. He'd passed gas so much that he was sure that the next time he did it, he would shit himself. "Say, Jake, fuck you pulling me down here for, man? I gotta get back to my borough."

"Jake? Who the hell is that? My name is Federal Agent Bishop, Kammron. You will address me as such."

Kammron hugged himself and began to rock in his chair. "Yeah, whatever, Dunn. What's the bidness?"

Agent Bishop flipped open Kammron's file and pulled out one picture of a deceased person after the next. When he finally got to Shana's, he slid it to the middle of the table, along with Shelly's. Shelly was Shana's older sister, and Kammron's ex. "These picture ring any bells?"

"Not them mafuckas over there, but I know dese hoes. That's Shelly, and that's Shana. I fucked both of them." Kammron sat back with a smile on his face.

Agent Bishop glared at him. He tapped his finger on Shana's picture. "Where were you on Thursday a month ago today, when Shana was killed?"

Kammron shrugged his shoulders. "Your guess is as good as mine because I don't know. When I found out that somebody had killed her, I was stunned."

"Stunned or saddened?" Bishop watched him closer.

"Stunned, never saddened. I ain't feel shit for that turncoat ass bitch. She got what she got. Life goes on." Kammron ran his hand over his face to wipe away the sweat. "How long am I going to be here? I got shit I gotta do."

Agent Bishop slid Shelly's picture in front of Kammron to see how he would react to it. "And what about her. Where were you approximately four months ago, at the time that she was killed?"

"Knowing me, I was probably fuckin' her li'l sister. Pussy way better, tighter, fresher. Why the fuck you asking me all of these questions?"

"Because before Shana was murdered we got a call from her about you. She told us that you killed her sister, and that if anything ever happened to her, we should come looking for you. We found that ironic, seeing as you are the father of her child. What woman would say somethin' like that unless it was the truth?"

"Don't know and don't give a fuck. That bitch was jaded. I dropped her and got to fuckin' wit a bitch that she trusted in and confessed all of her feelings and sins to. You know how hoes get."

"No, I wouldn't. I've been married for thirty five years." Bishop took the pictures and placed them back into a pile.

"To the same woman? Really?"

"Yes, really, but that has no relevance to this interrogation. Kammron, as of this moment, you are being looked at as the prime suspect for the murder of Shana and Shelly. And unless you can come up with some serious alibis real soon, you are going to spend the rest of your life in prison."

"No, I'm not. You got me fucked up. I ain't killed neither one of those bitches. You better check whatever technology you got to confirm that shit because I don't know what to tell you."

"Then where were you during their murders?"

"Muthafucka, I don't know. Where were you two years ago today?"

Agent Bishop glanced at the calendar. "I was at my oldest daughter's high school graduation. I wore a blue and white suit over Italian loafers. Your turn."

"Man, fuck you, because I don't know." A sharp pain shot through Kammron's stomach. He almost doubled over. He held his breath and closed his eyes for a moment. When he opened them again, Agent Bishop was placing new photographs on the table.

"Okay, Kammron, assuming you're telling the truth about the State's murder cases, it's now time that we switch over to why I am on your ass." He slid a picture of Jimmy across the table. Then Bonkers. Then Duke Da God sitting on top of a Ferrari. Last but not least, there was a picture of Kammron and Kamina, his attorney, standing in front of one of Kammron's trap houses in Harlem.

"Fuck you got pictures of all of my niggas and my lawyer for?"

"Because Kammron Giles-King, you and all of your boys are looking at the R.I.C.O. act."

Kammron's eyes got big as snow balls. "The R.I.C.O., for what?"

"Money laundering, slanging insane amounts of narcotics, murders, corrupt organization practices, there are so many charges set to come against you that you will never see the streets again. That you can bank on." It was Agent Bishop's turn to smile.

Kammron felt sicker. "Yo, what are you talkin' about?"

Agent Bishop spent the next hour showing Kammron both photos and video footage of his interactions with his many traps, his home boys, and he even had live footage of when Kammron and Bonkers were really in the field and handling jobs for Jimmy. The evidence was damning. Five times Agent Bishop was able to zoom directly into Kammron's face, so close he was able to make out the freckles on his cheeks. He was defeated. He started to imagine going through the drought of fighting off the heroin withdrawals, and he knew he wouldn't be able to do it.

"Who else have you arrested?" Kammron held his stomach tighter.

"Just you. That's all I feel like I need. We can always get the other guys five or ten years down the line. Make a big bust. There is no rush."

"What, why the fuck you coming to get me so early then?"

Agent Bishop stood up and shrugged his shoulders. "Because out of all of these guys, you are the most dangerous. We had to take you off of the streets. Had we not, New York's murder count would of rose more than it did during the COVID-19 pandemic." Agent Bishop grabbed the handle to the door and tucked the big file folder under his arm. "Besides, we have a better job of flipping those other guys. You're too tough for all of that. Aren't you?" He got ready to leave out.

Kammron dry heaved and fell to his knees. "Wait, what do you need me to do?" Kammron swallowed his spit. It tasted horrible to him. He needed his heroin. He felt weaker and weaker by the second. He was willing to do anything just to get out of that police station.

Agent Bishop came back into the room and slammed the door. "You know how we work in the Feds, Kammron. Why would you volunteer to do life in prison when you could pass that over to a friend? But then again, according to our audio on you, you're the king of Harlem. That along gets you sentenced as a kingpin. Unless..."

Kammron struggled to get back into his seat. He felt like his insides were being turned inside out. "Unless what?"

"Unless you work for us. These are our serious three targets." Agent Bishop pulled out a picture of Jimmy, once again, then Tristan, and lastly, Showbiz Vega. "Are you familiar with these two?" He pointed to Showbiz and Tristan.

"Those are the Vega boys. Showbiz calls himself the King of New York. They got the most clout so far, but that shit gon' change real soon. What about them?"

"We need Intel. We need to know how the Vegas run their operation. Theirs and Jimmy's. It has come to our attention that Jimmy is now receiving support from the islands. That's dangerous." He slammed a picture of Flocka on the table. "You know him?"

"His name is Flocka. He's one of our many connects. Say, Dunn, if I can help you bring down all four other mafuckas, what's in it for me? Do I get to keep my freedom?"

Agent Bishop was quiet for a while. "As far as we know, you are nothin' more than an employee of Jimmy's. That means that at the very most, you could go down for conspiracy. Now that carries a life sentence, but if you are cooperate, you could get your charges reduced all the way down to probation. You would have the federal government behind you, and seemingly the green light to take part in your business as usual, as long as you are working for the common good of the United States of America. You understand what I'm getting at?" He pulled out the pictures of Shana and Shelly again. "Somebody has to go down for these murders. If it isn't you, then it has to be somebody from your circle." He winked.

Kammron felt dizzy. "And if I agree to this shit, I can be released today?"

Agent Bishop grinned. "Well we wouldn't want the rest of your crew wondering where you are, now would we?"

"Hell nall. I'm in. I'll do whatever. Just get me the fuck out of here."

"Hold ya horses. There is a shit load of paperwork you'll have to sign, and then you can get back to your precious Harlem." Agent Bishop left the room with a sly smile on his face.

By the time he came back, Kammron had thrown up three times. He found him on his knees with cold sweat coming down the side of his face, and tears running down his cheeks. Kammron jumped up and snatched the pen from him. He signed every document that he needed to. Two hours after that, he was released and technically under federal property.

***

"Henny! Henny!" Kammron hollered, rushing into the house and falling to his knees. "Bitch, bring me my stash. I'm sick." He got up and took his shirt off. He could already feel the heroin flowing through his system. "Henny! You hear me?"

Bonkers came down the hallway with his arm around Henny's neck. She was dressed in a short gown that stopped just below her crotch. The gown was sheer enough for her nipples to be made out. "Damn, I see you have developed a whole ass habit ever since I was gone, huh, Kid?"

"Fuck is you doing in my house again, Bonkers? Don't you think you should've called?" Kammron shot back at him and rushed into this bedroom. He grabbed a shoebox from under the bed. He opened it and unwrapped the aluminum foiled China White. He pinched it and tilted his head back, sniffing hard through each nostril.

Bonkers stood at the doorway. He kissed Henny on the cheek. "Bitch, go shower. You stank."

Henny nodded and eased away from him, fearful of Kammron. What was he going to do, knowing that Bonkers had just screwed her? Would he kill her, or worse? At the very least, kick her to the curb? Those were the thoughts running through her head while she ran the shower water and got prepared to get into it.

Bonkers stepped further into the bedroom. "So I was talking to Yasmin, and she still refused to go into detail about what happened between you two. All she keeps saying is that she loves me, and that when I was down you held her down. I can't find a way to accept that."

Kammron wanted to shoot his heroin so badly but he knew that it would be a bad look in front of Bonkers, so he refrained. He relished in the feeling of the China White coursing through his system and was thankful that he was no longer locked at the police station. "Bonkers, I done already told you that I don't give a fuck about these hoes. Me and Yasmin did what we did out of necessity, and not disrespect. However, I apologize. However you wanna seek retribution, do what you gotta do. You still gon' be my nigga, and I'm still gon' be ready and willing to die for yo ass."

Bonkers came into the room and squatted down in front of Kammron. "I fucked Henny. Li'l bitch got a nice shot on her. Far as I'm concerned, we even." He held out his hand for Kammron to shake.

Kammron shook it and nodded. "Fuck my bitch, nigga, I don't save shit but money. You my family. We can pass these hoes around like recipes for all I care."

Bonkers laughed. "As much as I want to buss yo' ass, Killa, I can't. I feel like we blood. Besides, I've known you all of my life. I should already know that I can't bring a bitch around without you stuffing her ass. You've always been that way."

"Right, so why all of the sudden are you expecting me to change?"

"Because Yasmin made it seem like you took the pussy at first. I didn't know that it was mutual, and I still don't. For now, I'm just gon' keep her li'l ass put up. That way you ain't got no access to her until I find out if that boy is mine or yours. Yasmin doesn't wanna do a DNA test. She keeps asking me what's the use when our family is our family anyway."

Kammron looked him over from the corners of his eyes. "And you cool wit' that?"

"For now. That shit really ain't that important to me. Since she did her thing, I'ma do mine, too. But that ain't the reason I'm here. The reason I'm here tonight is because we gotta slide out to New Jersey and shut some shit down before it even comes this way toward Harlem."

"What are you talkin' about?" Kammron stood up, feeling breezy. He couldn't wait until Bonkers left so he could shoot his dope. The sounds of Henny's shower water played in the background.

"I got wind that those Yonkers boys have been using the Peter McGuire Projects as a safe post for their troops that are set to invade Harlem within a few weeks. I got some of our own troops from Harlem that's ready to roll across the bridge with us, too. Jimmy trying to get me to fuck wit him on this Queens endeavor as well. In fact, he is trying to give me Queens. I don't know what I'ma do just yet, though."

"Take it. Because ain't nobody finna have Harlem, other than Killa. I live and bleed Harlem. I always have and I always will, until the day they take the air out of my lungs."

Bonkers frowned at him. "Nigga I bleed Harlem just as much as you, if not more. You forget that I caught my first body in that bitch, way before you thought to pull the trigger on a nigga. Don't be making it seem like you got more of a stake in the borough than I do."

Kammron sneered at him. "I ain't say dat shit, you did. Queens seem more fitting for you, though. Whereas, Harlem already belongs to me. Every nigga that you see eating round dis bitch gotta pay homage to Killa Kam." Kam then closed his eyes and allowed for the heroin to course through his system. It only took him halfway to where he really needed to be.

Bonkers dusted off his red and white Dapper Dan fit, and shook his head at Kammron. "Anyway, I just wanted to tell you what was good before I went out and handled a li'l bidness on the front lines. I would invite you to come, but seeing as you got that shit all in your body, you might be more of a liability than an asset." Bonkers walked to the doorway of the hallway and laughed at Kammron. "Besides, Harlem is the most money-making borough of all the rest. I know you will never be able to take our homeland where it needs to be without me at the helms. Let's just keep that shit a buck." Bonkers left out of the den. "You need me, Kammron. My coma ain't change that shit."

Kammron wanted to get up and attack Bonkers verbally, but he figured that the longer he stayed and debated him, the longer it would take for Bonkers to leave. And the heroin was calling him like a thirsty one night stand. "Yeah, whatever, Dunn." Kammron waited until he heard Bonkers peel away from the curb before he pulled out his works and got it all ready. Ten minutes later, he was injecting the heroin into his system and groaning in euphoria.

Chapter 5

"Yo, I don't give a fuck what you talking about, Bishop. I'll wear the bug and all of that shit, but you finna allow me to trick this mafucka out." Kammron held up a chunky gold chain and looked it over with a smile on his face. He took his iced 'The Set' piece out of his Chanel knapsack and held it up for the jeweler to see. "Yo, I wanna cop this chain right here and I want this piece attached to it. How soon can you make this happen?"

The Puerto Rican jeweler looked both items over and shrugged his shoulders. "Give me a hour and I'll have you right."

"You hear that, Bishop? All the man needs is an hour, which means that you and I got time to get an understanding. Come on, let's go out here and get somethin' to eat."

Agent Bishop followed Kammron out onto a busy Seventh Ave, where they stopped at a hotdog stand. The sun was shining bright in the sky, though it was windy and chilly out. "Say, kid, let me get a hotdog. One of those beef ones." Kammron pulled out a hundred dollar bill and handed it to the Asian man that ran the hotdog cart.

Agent Bishop ordered a hotdog and wound up putting a bunch of condiments on it. By the time he was finished, it looked like he had done way too much. Relish was dripping all off of the bun. He opened his big mouth and bit a huge chunk from it.

Kammron was disgusted. "Word to Kathy, pig, you make these shits look nasty as hell." He threw his hotdog on the ground and kept walking.

Agent Bishop finished his hotdog. "You gotta set up a meeting with Jimmy, and you have to make a few purchases of the heroin that he got coming from overseas, at least five kilos. We aren't playing any games with him. We wanna get him for major drug trafficking, and hit him with king-pinning. In order to do that, the purchases have to be major, and outlandish. You up for the task?"

Kammron nodded. "Yeah, I don't give a fuck about Jimmy, or bringing his punk ass down. How soon do you need for these buys to take place?"

"Like yesterday. We got two hundred thousand in marked cash for you to purchase the drugs with, as well. It'll be a simple process, and we'll make sure that we are recording it all."

Kammron stopped at a soda pop machine and grabbed a Pepsi. He twisted the cap off of the twenty ounce bottle. "Wait, y'all ain't trying to bring his ass in right now, are you? I mean, I ain't about to be in the middle of a buy and y'all rush in on some indictment shit right there."

Agent Bishop wiped his fingers on a napkin. "You're dealing with the Feds, Kammron. What you're describing is a state level drug bust. This is federal. We accrue mountains of evidence before we indict. This is why we have a ninety plus margin of conviction rate, and growing. Nothing will take place on the night you buy the drugs, other than your purchase of them. We'll take them away from you and log them in as evidence and exhibits. It's a smooth process."

"Yeah, I hear you, white man. Anyway, when should this go down?"

"As soon as you can set up the meeting."

***

"Well, if ain't big bad Killa Kam from Harlem. The mafucka that don't need nobody, but all of the sudden need somebody. Welcome to Queens, nigga. It took you long enough to get here." Jimmy laughed, as he stepped aside and allowed for Kammron to walk into his three story red brick home.

Kammron looked him up and down and cruised past him, without shaking up or showing him any fake love. "Yo, them dread heads got you rocking that dreadlock shit now, too, huh, Jimmy? You might as well cross all the way over and start hollering that Rasta shit." Kammron snickered. He looked back at Jimmy.

Jimmy furrowed his eyebrows. "You ain't needed to holler at me in months, li'l nigga. Now, all of a sudden, you reach out. You must've heard about this sauce I been getting from the islands, huh? You come to capitalize off of my connect?"

"I heard you bringing in the best? That's all Harlem gon' ever get, as long as I'm king. That's why I come to fuck wit you."

"You ain't no muthafuckin king of Harlem, Kammron. Stop saying that shit. In order to be king, you gotta have them M's put up. You can't be closing in on a million and really think that you're doing something, because you're not."

"You don't know what I'm working wit', or who. And that's beside the point. I got four hundred thousand right here, and I'm trying to get right. Fuck wit me."

Jimmy laughed. "Yeah, you ain't on shit. I'll take this li'l four hunnit and blow that shit on a gold weekend in Vegas. What you tryna cop from me wit' this chump change."

"Twenty kilos. Since you be having that real green, though, thirty. I'm good for it." Kammron rubbed his nose and sniffed hard to clear out his nostrils, which had heroin residue inside of them. He looked around and admired Jimmy's ducked off pad. It was clean and cozy, with black leather furniture and paintings hung up on the walls.

"How the fuck you gon' say you the king when you coming to me and asking for favors? That make any sense to you?" Jimmy took a bottle of Moët off of his counter and drank from it.

"Nigga, it's four hundred thousand dollars in this bag. How the fuck that sound to you like I'm asking you for a favor?" Kammron wanted to blow Jimmy off the map with two shots to his dome, but knew that Agent Bishop and the feds were listening. Besides, he needed to use Jimmy in order to avoid the indictment that was coming to Harlem and the Vega Boys, alike.

Jimmy took a seat on the couch and crossed his legs. "Kammron, have a seat, li'l nigga."

"Yo, you already know I don't like when you get to hollering that li'l nigga shit. I'm a grown ass man. Fuck doing bidness wit you, or getting an understanding, if you can't respect and honor my gangsta." Kammron headed back toward the front door of Jimmy's pad.

"Instead of the twenty kilos, Kammron, on the strength of Harlem, I'ma give you forty, because I still got love for you, despite what you may be feeling in yo heart for a nigga. And besides, I don't give a fuck how major you think you is, you will always work under Jimmy the Capo." Jimmy stood up. "You got that?"

Kammron clenched his jaw tightly. "Yeah, nigga, I got that. Let's finish this bidness so I can get back to my muthafuckin borough."

***

Bonkers came into the house and was graced with the aroma of fried chicken, pinto beans, white rice, cornbread, collard greens, and German chocolate cake. When he stepped

Coke Kings 4

into the kitchen, he slid his arms around Yasmin's waist and kissed her neck. "What it do, boo?"

Yasmin jumped and then calmed down after hearing Bonkers' voice. Him being out of his coma was still new to her. "Hey, baby, how was your day?"

"Long, but it's over now." He kissed her neck, and looked on the stove. She was stirring the pot of greens and adding her special spices.

"What you do, cook up the whole house?" He laughed and kissed her again.

"The doctor's said that you need to put your weight back on. You lost thirty unhealthy pounds while you were in your coma so I'm trying to make sure that you are eating a nice meal every single night. A meal that's gon' put some meat on them bones again. I liked that stocky look. I don't know what this look is." She smiled and kept cooking. "Where were you?"

"Really, we doing that?" He slipped from behind her and opened the refrigerator door.

Yasmin got the greens to where she needed them to be before she closed the pot with the lid. "Shy, you don't think I have a right to ask you where you were? Aren't we together?"

"Yeah, we together for Yazzy and the baby. But are we really together for us? That's what you really have to ask yourself." He picked up a bottle of apple juice and turned it up.

Yasmin sighed and shook her head. "It's to the point now that you're either going to forgive me for my transgressions or leave me altogether. I swear, every time I feel like you and I are making progress, we wind up falling back into this sphere of where we are now. Damn, I'm sorry for fuckin' up. I love you. I wanna have a family with just you. Can you please let me live?" She placed her hand on her hip and zoomed in to his neck. "What the fuck is that?" She pointed at the right side of his neck. "Come here."

Bonkers stupidly walked over to her. "What's good?"

Yasmin held him by the chin and tilted his head sideways. She rubbed the passion mark that Henny had left on him while he was stroking her ass down. "Who the fuck been sucking on yo neck, Bonkers?"

"What? Nobody. Ain't no mafucka been sucking on my neck." He walked away from her and headed into the bathroom. He flipped on the light and leaned his head to the side so he could view the right side. He saw the purplish red mark right away. He scratched at it. "Man, you tripping. That ain't come from nobody sucking on my mafuckin' neck. It comes from me scratching shit all day because you got me using that cheap ass Irish Spring. You already know my skin is sensitive. I can't fuck wit nothin' but Dove or Lever 2000." He scratched it some more.

Yasmin looked him over suspiciously. "So where were you before you got back here?"

"Trapping. I'm trying to get shit in order wit' Queens before I move some more of my loyal troops from Harlem out there. It's a process."

"I don't know what you see as loyal, but when you were down, you didn't have more than three visitors. I don't understand why you can keep going along and trusting all of these dudes, but I'm telling you that you ain't doing nothing but swimming in a pool of snakes. That goes for your brother, Jimmy, too. He ain't right."

"Oh yeah, well, what makes you say that?"

"Because I can tell that he didn't expect for you to pull through. He didn't ask me if I needed help with Yazzy one time. He got all of that got damn money and he didn't give us a crumb while you were in your coma."

"Maybe if he did then you wouldn't've had to turn to Kammron, huh?" Bonkers scoffed and walked out of the bathroom. "Shorty, if I find out that you weren't doing shit but chasing that bag while I was down, we gon' have a serious ass problem. Jimmy don't owe you shit."

"Clearly not his niece, either. The only person that reached for us while you were in your coma was Kammron. As much as I hate him, I gotta give him his due. We didn't want or need for shit. He's more of a brother to you than Jimmy will ever be. That move to Queens is stupid. It's ill advised, and it's going to be the death of you. Mark those words. Dinner will be served in twenty minutes." She brushed past him and went back to cooking.

Bonkers stood in the hallway with his head down. He thought about Kammron, then Jimmy, then Queens. He took a deep breath and sighed. "I just had to wake up to all of this madness. I don't know how to trust." He said low enough for only himself to hear it. He left out of the hallway and knocked on Yazzy's bedroom door.

"Who is it?" She asked, typing away on her iPad.

"Yazzy, it's daddy. Can I come in?"

She nodded. "Yes, daddy."

Bonkers pulled open the door and picked her up. She dropped her iPad on the bed and started laughing, wrapping her arms around his neck. Bonkers kissed her cheek and kept his lips planted to her skin. "I love you, Yazzy. I mean that with every fiber of my being. No matter what takes place with your mother and I, you should always know that you are my heart and soul. Do you understand me?"

"Yes, daddy." She kissed his cheek and hugged him tightly.

"Never forget, baby." Bonkers looked down on her, and then closed his eyes while hugging her to his body until the ill feelings that he had roaming through his mind about Yasmin and Kammron subsided. Then he was able to put on a fake smile and attend dinner with his family.

Chapter 6

Duke sat in the middle of the black Chevy Astro van with a hundred round Draco on his lap and two .45 pistols in his holsters. His red bandana was pulled up his face, just under his eyes. The van was loaded up with ten of his best shooters from Uptown. Duke had personally picked each man for this particular endeavor. He looked around the van with the heroin flowing heavily through his system. His eyes were low and furious. "Say, shorty, hit me with a few lines of dat coke. I'm too mafuckin' low."

Juanita, a young project goddess from the Harlem River Houses, hurried from the passenger's seat and pulled out two vials of pure cocaine. She held one under Duke's nostrils and allowed for him to snort it.

Duke took both vials and felt his heart begin to beat rapidly. He sniffed and bucked his eyes. "Yeah, muthafucka. There we go. Y'all ready to do this shit? Huh? Y'all ready to fuck over these Jersey boys?"

The killas in the van began to nod and cheer loudly. The van rocked on its suspensions as the driver drove down the long winding alley that led to the Peter McGuire Projects. When the Project buildings came into view, she slowed down and pulled up her red bandana.

Duke docked his Draco. "Awright, muthafuckas. Everybody gon' follow my lead. When we get in this bitch, we gon' kill everything moving. This is a no mercy mission. Every last one of these mafuckas that's about to meet these bullets is prepared to move out to Harlem by the end of the month and take over the blocks where you eat and were bred at. We can't allow that. It's money and supremacy over everything. Let's go in here and handle this business."

***

Duke came to the back door of the project building and was met by a tall dark skinned female with way too much make up on. She stuck her head out of the door and looked both ways. When she saw how many people were beside Duke, she knew that it was about to go down. Duke handed her ten thousand dollars and she ran out of the building.

Duke waved for his troops to follow him inside. They rushed in and up the stairs to the ninth floor, which was used for cooking up dope and mixing up large quantities of China White. To Duke's amazement, every door on the floor was opened, just like the dark skinned female had promised him they would be. Kammron told him that inside of each apartment were Jason's workers and shooters, and that he should go in with no mercy. And that's what he intended to do.

***

The dark skinned woman ran full speed down the alley. She looked over her shoulder over and over again, waiting to hear the gunshots that were inevitable. When she heard the first series, she stopped in her tracks to see what she could see. Juanita crept out of the garage and slipped behind her. She placed her .9 millimeter to the back of her head and pulled the trigger.

Boom!

The bullet punched its way into the dark skinned woman's skull and knocked her brain out the front of her face. She screamed and did a one eighty turn. She reached up for Juanita. Juanita stood over her and aimed at her face.

Boom! Boom!

The dark skinned woman jerked on the pavement twice before her soul escaped her body. She lay with her eyes wide open. Her last sights were of Juanita taking the ten thousand dollars that was saturated in her blood off of her body.

***

Duke took a step back and kicked in the apartment door. He rushed inside, and as soon as he saw the first person, his assault rifle was spitting rapidly. The bullets zipped across the room, striking one dope boy after the next. Duke watched the holes fill up their bodies. They fell over tables and struggled to get out of the way.

When he started shooting, his troops started to do the same thing. In a matter of seconds, there were ten dead bodies on the floor, leaking. Duke stood over each body with his hand gun and over-killed them to make sure that they were deceased. Then he ran out of the apartment and joined his shooters in the next one, where he unloaded clip after clip with no regard.

The smell of gun smoke and blood excited him. He cheesed under his red bandana and felt a surge of adrenalin. By the time they left the ninth floor, they had killed fifteen men and only lost two of their own. Duke considered it a good job, and as they drove back to Harlem, he got on the phone with Kammron, giving him the entire update on the mission. Unbeknownst to him, Kammron was recording the entire phone call for safe keeping.

***

Kammron stepped into his home with two duffel bags that held the shipment from Jimmy. Forty kilos of pure heroin that

Jimmy had promised him. Agent Bishop had only wanted Kammron to make the deal for five of the kilos. Kammron was thinking that he would give the man ten, and keep the other thirty. He didn't care how Bishop felt about it either. Kammron was still forced to find a way to survive, even though he was working with the feds. He closed the door behind him.

When he heard a female laugh, which was followed by another, he squinted his eyes and peeked down the hallway.

"Henny? Shorty, who the fuck you got in my house?"

Henny came walking down the short hallway wearing a pair of Daisy Dukes that were all up in her crevice. Her thick thighs jiggled with each step that she took. "Well I'm still waiting for my sister and my cousin to get here. But in the meantime, I found you another female that went to my school. She is a few years younger than me, and she just ran away from home because her mother kept trying to beat on her and shit." She looked over her shoulder. "Reyanna, come here and meet my daddy."

Reyanna came down the hallway apprehensively. She'd heard a lot about Kammron, and none of it was good. He was a deadly legend around Harlem. All of the girls were raised to stay away from him. She stepped into the living room with her head lowered. She stepped beside Henny.

Henny smacked her lips. "Hell n'all, girl, I know yo ass ain't shy?" She rolled her eyes.

Kammron grabbed a hold of Reyanna's wrist and pulled her to him. She was five feet two inches tall, thick, with caramel skin and almond shaped eyes. Her hair was thick and wavy. It flowed down her back and was in desperate need of maintenance. Kammron made her do a twirl so he could check out all of her body. Her ass poked out inside of the short skirt that Henny had allowed her to borrow. Kammron gripped her ass.

"You like her, daddy? Did I do good?" Henny asked, kissing Kammron on the cheek.

"Yeah, shorty, this li'l bitch cold. Say, shorty, what type of dope yo mama do?" Kammron asked.

"She messes with that heroin real tough, and every now and then, when she can afford it, she cops that Magic stuff from those Yonkers hustlers across St. Nicholas Ave."

"Un-huh. You sho she ain't gon' come looking for you?" Kammron eyed her thick thighs and felt his piece getting hard. He knew she was young and fresh. That was exciting to him.

"My mother doesn't care about nobody but herself. As long as she stay high, she couldn't care less what goes on in the world." Reyanna lowered her head again. She couldn't bring herself to look into Kammron's eyes.

"What about yo old man? What that nigga be on?" Kammron ran his fingers through her hair. There was light streaks of dirt on her face.

"I don't know who my daddy is, and I'm pretty sure that my mother doesn't either, but it's all good. I don't wanna know who he is if he ain't reached for me this far." Reyanna looked over at Henny. Henny stood a safe distance away. She didn't want to get in the mix with Kammron while he appraised a new girl.

"Well, fuck yo' mama and yo' daddy. You hear me. I'm daddy now, and if you fuckin' wit me, I'ma make sure that you got everything that you need and more. I can look at yo li'l ass and tell that you been neglected a lot, ain't you?" Kammron rubbed down her back and stopped at her waist.

"Yeah, but I ain't gon' complain. I'ma keep dealing with whatever cards that God deals me. Life is what it is." She looked into Kammron's eyes. "Why do everybody say that you're crazy and to stay away from you?"

Kammron laughed. "Because I am crazy and you should stay away from me, especially if you wanna be a bum for the rest of your life." He leaned his face down and kissed her neck. "Anybody ever told you that yo li'l ass strapped?"

She shrugged her shoulders. "If they did, I wasn't listening. Words don't mean nothin' to me, especially if the person that's using them doesn't contribute to what's going inside of my belly. I'm tired of starving, and I'm tired of being broke. You want me to call you daddy, but what are you going to change about my situation?"

Kammron placed his forehead on her smaller one. "That depends if you plan on falling under Killa Kam, or not."

She eyed him. "Let's say that I am, then what?"

"Then you would be like my li'l baby. The burden of you is solely on my shoulders. I'll make sure you stay fed, rocking the latest fashions, and dicked down. That's definitely a part of the program." Kammron rubbed all over her chunky booty and cuffed the cheeks.

"What if I say that I'm too young to be thinking about anything like that? I ain't never been with a grown ass man before. I'm scared." She placed her left hand on his shoulder.

Kammron was rock hard already. He kissed her neck first and then bit into it. She moaned. He sucked it and slipped his hand between her legs from the back. He eased up the short skirt and dipped his hand into her, rubbing over her pussy lips. They were fat with little hairs on them. He opened the lips with his fingers and slipped his middle digit into her hole. She was tight and barely allowed him entrance before she pushed on his shoulder and backed up. Kammron sniffed his finger.

"Say, Henny, she's staying wit' us. I want you to give her a bath and put her on some of that sexy ass lingerie you got until I'm able to order her her own shit. Hurry up, she sleeping wit me tonight."

"What about me?" Henny was already feeling jealous.

"What about you?" Kammron picked up his duffel bags.

"I don't wanna be left out. After all, she is my friend," Henny whined.

Kammron dropped his bags. He walked up to Henny with a frown on his face. "Aw, so you gon' play wit' me already in front of this li'l bitch, huh? Awright then." He grabbed Henny by the neck and lifted her into the air, taking her feet off of the ground. Henny kicked her feet wildly. Kammron squeezed harder. "See, Reyanna, don't get fucked up like this bitch. All you gotta do is listen and this won't happen to you. Kammron don't feel no fuckin' emotions. Listen and you get whatever you want, don't, and I'ma get on yo monka-ass. You understand me? Say yes before I kill this bitch," he snarled.

"Yes!" Reyanna hollered.

Kammron choked Henny for a while longer before he dropped her to the ground. "Now get yo' ass up and do like I say. Fuck wrong wit chu?"

Henny got up, holding her neck. She grabbed Reyanna's hand and pulled her down the hallway. "Come on, girl, before he fuck me up some more. I'm sorry, daddy! Please know that I'm sorry," she hollered over her shoulder.

T.J. Edwards

Chapter 7

Kammron stepped into the boardroom and dropped the ten kilos of heroin that he'd gotten from Jimmy on to the table. "Huh, man. You asked for five and I'm giving you ten." Kammron sat back and sipped on a bottle of vitamin water that was mixed with three Percocet Sixties, pink Mollie, and two Oxytocins. He was high as a kite and ready to get back home so he could fuck Reyanna into oblivion.

Agent Bishop stood up and surveyed the packages of dope. He placed them side by side, and nodded his head. "This is only ten, where are the rest of them?" He scratched the bald spot that was in the middle of his head.

Kammron sparked a blunt stuffed with Syracuse Orange. He puffed off of the weed and blew the smoke toward the ceiling. "Muthafucka, you asked me for five bricks. I'm doing you a solid and giving you ten. That's basically twenty a kee. You ain't finna go nowhere in New York and get a mafucka to sell you a pure brick of that Island shit for twenty a piece."

Unbeknownst to Agent Bishop, Kammron had already stepped on the dope a whole bunch and given the feds a poor quality of the narcotics that he'd received from Jimmy. The dope went from ninety five percent pure all the way down to thirty percent. Kammron didn't care. He didn't give a fuck about the Feds and wasn't interested in Jimmy's dope sitting in an evidence locker when it could've been on the streets of Harlem, making him hundreds of thousands of dollars.

Agent Bishop waved his hand and another agent came into the room and grabbed the heroin off of the table before disappearing. Bishop made sure that the man was gone before he sat on the edge of the table and took off his glasses. He lowered his head and rubbed his eyes. "Kammron, this is not how things go. You see, I have people that I have to answer to. We heard on audio that Jimmy was supposed to give you forty kilos of heroin. This is only ten. Where are the other thirty?"

"Jimmy only gave me ten. The same ten he gave me I'm giving y'all. Y'all been tailing him for a while now, I am sure. Y'all should know that that muthafucka ain't never been a man of his word."

Agent Bishop rubbed his eyes some more before putting his glasses back on. "So this is the angle that you're going to play, huh?"

"I ain't playin' shit. I'm telling you what he gave me. Like I said before, you wanted five, and I gave you double that. Instead of treating me like I did somethin' wrong, you should be praising me for doubling what you set out for me to get."

"Come on now, Kammron. Knock it the fuck off. You're wearing my patience real thin," Bishop snapped.

"Who the fuck you hollering at, white man?" Kammron stood up.

"You, motherfucker! You think I was born yesterday? I know that Jimmy gave you forty kilos. There was no reason for him to give you two duffel bags if he only supplied you with ten bricks. That's nonsense." He started to turn as red as a lobster.

"I don't give a fuck what you talkin' bout. I gave you what he gave me. That's the best I can do for you. Let me know when you need some other shit handled. Until then, I'ma lay back and fuck wit some fresh hoes. You need to go and pop a bottle, Bishop. You shot for five, and pulled back ten. That's really sayin' somethin'." Kammron headed toward the exit of the upstairs office.

"Kammron Giles-King, I swear, if you leave out of that door, I'm going to haul your ass into the station tonight and book you in for breach of federal contract, and for all of those murders that I personally know that you committed. You black son of a bitch, the next time you see the outside of a prison is when we ship you all the way to California. Now sit your ass down. Now!" Agent Bishop stood with his hand over his service weapon.

Kammron stopped and turned around with a wicked smile on his face. "Cool." He sat in a chair at the far end of the board meeting table. "What the fuck you want, man?"

Agent Bishop trailed his fingers through his hair again. He was sweating. "Okay, you wanna keep the thirty kilos of heroin? Fine. But you're going to have to give me something."

"I ain't got no thirty kilos, but whatever. What else do you want from me?" Kammron puffed off of his blunt and inhaled his weed smoke deeply.

"There was a brutal mass murder earlier tonight over in Camden, New Jersey, one in which fifteen plus people were killed. The cameras were able to catch a glimpse of two of the vans, and both of them report to residents that are from Harlem, which leads us to believe that the people who did these heinous murders are also from Harlem. Now we can't pin them on you, because we've been tracking you since early this morning, in preparation for this transaction with Jimmy. But I am sure that you know who did this. Don't you?"

Kammron pulled on his beard hair and looked Agent Bishop over from the side of his eyes. "Suppose I could find out who did it, what's it worth to you?"

Agent Bishop walked around the table and toward Kammron until he was standing in front of him. "There were fifteen people killed, Kammron. That's considered a terrorist attack."

"And once again, I'm asking you, what is it worth to you?"

Agent Bishop was surging with anger. "Fuck! Okay, this indictment news is set to wrap up within the next few months.

61

Harlem is going to be flooded with cops and every form of law enforcement, making it hard for the dope sellers to push their products. We're also going to be doing a lot of stop and frisking. Governor Cuomo has already approved these measures. If you give me a few leads that will lead to the arrest of the person or persons that committed these acts of terrorism, I will see to it that your sections of Harlem aren't tampered with, and also that this Intel is added to your case for immunity when the pending charges that are coming against you are brought down. You won't serve more than a week inside. You have my word on that."

Kammron stubbed out his blunt on the table of the board room. "I'll see what I can do, no promises." He jumped up. "Anything else?"

Bishop sighed. "No, Kammron, you're dismissed.

***

Reyanna opened Kammron's bedroom door fresh out of the shower. She was wearing a tight, form fitting, red lace nightgown that stopped just above her crotch. She eased into the room just as Kammron was sliding his pistol under the pillow. She smiled shyly. "I'm here."

Kammron turned around and nodded. "Hell yeah, you are, ma. Come mere." He met her halfway. His arms circled her waist. He slid his hands down until they we're cuffing her fat ass cheeks. He squeezed them and kissed her lips. She was shaking.

"I-I-I'm not gon' lie and say I ain't scared, because I am. I ain't never did this before."

Kammron licked her lips. "It's all good, li'l baby, because I have and I'ma make sure I break you off the Harlem way. A bitch as thick as you gotta be fucked by a savage first and foremost." He slipped his hands under her skirt and into her thong, playing over her sex lips.

"Mmm, wait, Kammron. What about Henny?" She held his wrist.

Kammron sucked her neck and licked all over the thick vein there. "What about Henny?" He peeled open her pussy lips and rotated his finger around her entrance. She slowly began to get wet. He sucked harder on her neck, causing her nipples to spike.

"Can she come in here with me? I'm scared."

Kammron stopped and picked her up by the waist. He tossed her backward on the bed and pulled off his black beater. He was tatted all over. Two gold ropes swung on his neck. The light reflected off of his ice. "Shorty, you wit Killa. Henny can't save you now."

He yanked up her gown and placed it around her waist. He licked over the crotch of her panties and stuffed the material into her sex lips. Her brown folds appeared on each side. They were naked after Henny shaved them for her. Kammron yanked the material to the side and opened her wide. Her pink glistened and oozed down to her ass cheek. "Damn, for you to be just a shorty, this pussy fat." He kissed the pearl.

Reyanna arched her back and moaned. "Unh! Kammron, please let Henny come in here. What if I can't take that big... Uhhhh!" She moaned and shivered.

Kammron was licking and sucking her clitoris. He slurped loudly. So loud that Henny was able to hear every suck and flick of Kammron's tongue. When he stuck his tongue inside of her as far as it could go and diddled her pearl tongue, Reyanna screamed and came, squirting her juices at Kammron. He placed his mouth over her geyser and sucked until it became too sensitive, and then she began to push him away.

Reyanna scooted backward on the bed and stuck her hand between her thighs. She struggled to catch her breath. Her eyes were bucked wide open. "What did you just do to me?" Her fingers slipped between her slit rubbing her clit. Juices dripped off of her fingers.

Kammron stood at the foot of the bed stroking his dick. He pumped it at a moderate pace. "Shorty, get yo ass over here and let me introduce you to this grown shit. Second lesson, you finna learn how to suck a nigga. Come here."

Reyanna crawled across the bed and stopped on all fours. She sat on her bottom and scooted forward. "Yes, daddy?"

"First, lay back and let me look between yo thick li'l thighs. I still can't believe you dis mafuckin' strapped. Fuck they putting in the water dese days? Damn." Her bald pussy lips were plump. They looked good shaved. She was fresh. He could still taste her on his tongue. He stroked his dick faster, until it was standing up like a dark brown cucumber.

"I don't know," Reyanna's eyes got bigger and bigger the more Kammron's piece extended. She couldn't imagine herself being able to take what he had to offer. That seemed like an impossible task.

Kammron placed his fingers in her hair and guided her toward his dick. "Check dis out, shorty, don't hit my shit, and don't scrape my shit with those teeth. If you do, I'ma beat yo li'l ass, that's word to Harlem. You understand that?"

"Okay." She leaned her head forward and wound up with her lips right on the tip of it.

"Awright, lick around my head like it's the top of a ice cream cone."

"Like this?" Reyanna held his thick monster with her left hand and licked all around his plump head. It was salty and rubbery.

Kammron reached across her back and dipped his fingers into her pussy from behind. She was oozing. "Yeah, now suck just on that part that you kicked while I get this li'l baby pussy ready to be beat in. Damn, you working wit' a lot." He trembled at the feel of her sucking him into her mouth. "Unnn."

Reyanna sucked him slow at first. He guided her head with his hand, and then he was humping into her mouth, while standing on his tippy toes. She gagged and scooted backward. Every time she moved backward, his fingers went deep into her young pussy. She groaned and sucked him harder, thankful that Henny had given her some Mollie just before Kammron arrived. The drug was starting to kick in. Her nipples extended. Her pussy began to ooze, while her clitoris jumped and throbbed. She sucked Kammron hungrily.

Kammron pumped his hips faster and faster, while fingering her. When he felt that he was getting ready to splash, he pulled out and aimed his head at her face. "Unh fuck, li'l bitch." His seed shot and landed on her face with jet after jet. He nutted and smashed his head against her cheeks, while his seed spit out of him. Then he angled it so that she was sucking him again. Her slurping got louder and louder. Now her box was dripping wet. He could smell her and it drove him crazy.

Reyanna jagged him while she sucked him at full speed. When he was rock hard again, she pulled him out of her mouth and beat him off. "Did I do good, Kammron, I mean, daddy?" His piece continued to throb in her hand.

Kammron pulled his fingers out and sucked them into his mouth. "Hell yeah." He climbed onto the bed and pushed her onto her back, while he felt between her thighs. His middle fingers slipped between her folds again. He fingered her fast, pulled them out, and rubbed them all over her lips. "Smell yo self, shorty." He guided his dick into her, while pressing her knees to her chest. He sank in and slammed home hard.

"Uhhhhhhh shoot!" Reyanna tried to push him off of her. "Please!"

Kammron felt how tight her pussy was and it excited him. He cocked his back and slammed home again and again. He got a steady rhythm and proceeded to dick her down as only a savage could. The headboard tapped against the wall loudly. Reyanna was trying to get from under him. She threw the blanket off of the bed and dug her nails into his waist. This only excited Kammron.

"Daddy! Daddy! Shoot! Shoot! Uhhhh fuck! Wait! You're killing me. It hurts... Uhhhh, shit, it's too much!"

"Dis Harlem, shorty! Dis Harlem. I'm the king! I'm the king!" He growled. He pressed her knees tighter to her breasts and fucked her at full speed.

Reyanna screamed and tried to catch her breath. She could feel Kammron hitting her G spot over and over. Her eyes rolled into the back of her head. She sat up and licked his face. She didn't know why she did it, but she did. Then she fell back and screamed louder. "Daddy! Dadddddddeeeeeee!" She screamed and came, shaking uncontrollably.

Kammron kept pounding away. She was hot and gushy. Her insides gripped him like a fist. He stopped and ripped her gown open. The sound of the linen tearing was loud in the room. Her perky breasts spilled out. He squeezed them and sucked one nipple into his mouth, and then the other, while he fucked into her. He lifted his head up. "You gon' be my main bitch. This pussy fresh. I can see that." He dug deeper. "You hear me?"

"Unh! Unh! Un-huh! Yes, daddy!" She arched her back again and Kammron sank deeper. He pulled all the way back and slammed back into her. Her eyes crossed as another massive orgasm rocked her. She bit into his shoulder and came hard.

Henny came into the room with her left hand under her gown and in her panties. "Daddy, what about me? Please don't forget about me." She hurried and climbed on the bed. She licked up and down Kammron's back, before biting it.

"Mmm, bitch. You are so hard-headed. He stuffed Reyanna as far as he could go. She screamed, and he came in large spurts back to back. He pulled out and came all over her titties and stomach. "Open them thighs, li'l baby, and let me see that fresh pussy."

Reyanna laid back, breathing hard. She opened her thighs wide for him. Her fingers pulled her young nipples. She couldn't believe that he had been inside of her with all of that between his legs. Sweat slid down the side of her face.

Kammron came in a silky line over her folds. They glistened with his cum. He rubbed it all around with the head of his dick. "Hell yeah. You broke the mold wit' this bitch right here, Henny."

Henny kissed his neck. She felt jealous and left out. "Daddy, do you got somethin' left in the tank for me?"

Kammron slipped out of the bed and stretched his arms over his head. "Time is money. You hoes can play for a minute. I gotta buss a few moves. I'm good for now."

"Aw-uh." Henny punched the bed. She glared at the back of his head as he walked out of the bedroom. Then she shot daggers down at Reyanna, but she was curled into a ball already drifting off to sleep. Her body shined with Kammron's nut all over her. "This some bullshit."

T.J. Edwards

Chapter 8

Kammron took the pure shipment from Jimmy and flooded Harlem, alongside Duke Da God. In a matter of three weeks, they had copped an additional eighty birds from Jimmy and sewed up the borough like never before.

Duke opened fifty trap houses all around Harlem and had thirty of their workers trapping off of their cellphones. Those particular dope boys rolled all around the borough, answering and taking orders from dope addicts that called in or hit them up online. Duke made sure that the operation ran smoothly on all fronts, while Kammron sat back and oversaw everything.

In addition to putting numerous dope boys on, Kammron, hired an equal amount of dope girls that were dead set on checking a bag. Whether they worked the strip clubs and sold their product to other dancers, or customers that frequented the club, he didn't care, as long as he was getting rid of his shipments quickly and precisely. Every time he copped from Jimmy, he checked a few bricks into Agent Bishop and kept the rest.

Kammron took to having a few of his shooters pull jobs and gave them code words. He made them refer to him as Jimmy, and he constantly asked them, over and over, who they were loyal to, and they would always say Jimmy. Then he would have them go and gun down rival dope boys and report that information back to Agent Bishop, along with the recording of them pledging their loyalties to him, though using Jimmy's name.

***

A month after Kammron and Duke copped a hundred and fifty uncut bricks of West Indies heroin from Jimmy and his

Bryd Gang crew, Duke introduced Kammron to his cousin, Juelz.

It was a warm night in April. That morning Duke and Kammron had sat back and counted three million dollars apiece, using money machines, with the help of both Henny and Reyanna. Duke took a million away from the trap and Kammron put two million up in his safe, already figuring out how he was going to wash it clean. He had always been taught that Uncle Sam had to get his money no matter what. Kammron was a beast with flowing his cash through an assortment of businesses within Harlem. He didn't gamble with other boroughs. Harlem was his home and the only place that would ever see his dough.

They were sitting inside of Duke's black on black Phantom, sipping Lean, when Duke brought Juelz up. "Say, Kammron, now that a mafucka is making a few M's, I think it's time that I introduce you to my cousin, Juelz."

Kammron sipped out of his bottle and eyed Duke from the side of his eyes. "Fuck I wanna meet yo cousin for?"

"Cause, nigga, first off, he's my blood, and second off, that nigga is a real live hitta."

Kammron shrugged his shoulder. "I am, too, fuck that mean?"

"Yo, Juelz is from Chicago. He run with another nigga down here by the name of T.J. Them niggas get to that paper just like we do, but they specialize in that murder shit. Seeing as we got plenty mafuckas around New York that's trying to fuck in our bidness and give us unnecessary competition, I think it's time that we start putting that bag up on they head and moving they ass around the smart way. What you think?"

Kammron scratched his inner forearm and looked over to Duke. "What is the price tag for a body?"

"Fifteen gees a head, more than four at twelve a piece. Dig this, I got the drop on Jason and P. I found out that them niggas be chilling at a barbershop over in Newark, New Jersey. That nigga Jason got a jaded ass baby mother. He got her sister pregnant with twins. Yeah, nigga, she spilled all of those beans. Anyway, I can have my Chicago niggas go and face paint they ass with no problem. Juelz on standby right now. All you gotta do is let me give them the contract."

"I been in the game ever since I was thirteen years old and never once have I ever depended on a nigga to whack somethin' fa me. I'm a technical foul shooter. That means that I shoot my own shots and get the ball back." He sipped some more of his Lean. He was getting low.

"Yeah, well now you ain't gotta do all of that shit because you got M's. You can hire a mafucka to do yo light work. I want to employ these niggas under the set. I always wanna put some of that Ponchie shit in the Midwest. If we can break into Chicago with this work, nigga, we can be one step closer to being Coke Kings."

Kammron lit up. "That market open?"

"Hell yeah, it is, and I got them in through Juelz. We throw them a bone and they gon' throw us a whole ass dinosaur.

"I'll tell you what, Duke, set it up and make it happen. I'll fly them niggas out here personally. Let me know when you are ready and it's a done one. Word up."

"Say no mo'."

***

Jason sat back in the barber chair while his uncle edged him up. The clippers hummed against his forehead. "Yo, you're shaking like crazy, Lester. I think it's getting to that time that me and P are about to have to find another barber, word up." He laughed.

Lester held his head straight and made sure that he was still again before he began to line him. "Been cutting hair for thirty years and been shaking for ten. I ain't never fucked you up and I don't plan on doing it no time soon. Just be still and let me do what I do."

"Yeah, whatever. Yo, P, what time them Queens niggas supposed to be here to drop off that shit? We got some other stuff to handle as soon as I'm done getting right."

P leaned over the pool table and shot the eight ball into the left corner pocket. He glanced down at the Patek on his left wrist. "They should be pulling up any minute now." He slid the stick onto the pool table and walked to the front door. He glanced out of it, shielding his eyes from the sun. Then he stepped outside so he could see better.

It was a bright and sunny day. The barbershop was located on Martin Luther King Drive, which was a busy street in Newark. Cars sped up and down it until they were sometimes forced to stop at the traffic lights. He stepped onto the curb and looked both ways. Out of irritation, he picked up his phone and called Jimmy.

Jimmy picked up on the third ring. "What it do, Fleet?"

"Where yo' droppers at, man? These mafuckas are twenty minutes late. That's bad bidness, Jimmy, and you know it." P continued to look up and down the busy Martin Luther King Drive.

"Yo, chill, kid. I'ma hit blood nem up and see what's the hold up. As soon as I know, I'ma text you."

"Nall, nigga, don't text me. Make that shit happen." P hung up the phone and stepped in front of the barbershop to smoke a cigarette, when Juelz bent the corner and slowly slid the car in front of the barbershop. P remained on the wall with his nostrils flared.

T.J. stuck his head out of the window. He was caramel skinned with waves. His eyes were low and focused. "Say, Shorty, what it do?"

P placed his hand under his shirt and made his way to the car. He leaned down and looked inside of it. "Who you li'l niggas looking for?"

"Yo', we from New York, we got bidness for Jimmy. You P, or are you Jason?"

"I'm P, and only my nigga day ones call him by his government. Call the homie Jada, and not Jason. Y'all got the shit?" P looked both men over carefully.

"In the trunk. Five hundred thousand dollars and ten bricks of that island shit, just like you ordered." Juelz spoke up.

"It took you niggas long enough. Come on, follow me inside." P headed toward the barbershop entrance.

***

T.J. dropped the duffel bag on the pool table and stood in front of it. He eyed the three men inside of the shop with a laser-like focus. He assessed the threat level and kept his eyes pinned on P because P kept his hand under his shirt at all times.

Jason sat in the barber's chair, getting his haircut finished. "Jimmy don't discipline mafuckas in his outfit when they late like you two niggas are?"

T.J. shrugged his shoulders. "I don't know, that ain't my bidness to tell. However, which one of you is Jason? Is it you that's talking to me, or is it the one cutting the hair?"

Jason mugged him from the chair. "Nigga, I'm Jason. What, you don't know a Don when you see one?"

"Aw n'all, that ain't the case. Plus, I ain't seen you before. I just wanted to make sure, though. Say, bruh, so that's P then."

With blazing speed, T.J. came from under his shirt with two twin .40 Blockas that were already cocked. He stepped up to Jason and placed both barrels to his face. "Kammron sends his regards."

Boom! Boom! Boom! Boom!

Jason felt the bullets burn holes into his face. The flash was bright. He tried to move and felt the heat from his own brain particles dripping down his neck. He fell backward in the chair on his way to death. T.J. stood over him and popped four more holes into his face to make sure that he was a goner.

Before P could up his weapon, Juelz was bucking with a lethal intent. Juelz's first bullets caught P in the side of the neck. They zipped into his throat and knocked huge chunks out of it. P dropped his gun and fell to the floor, trying to hold his neck as blood gushed through his fingers. Juelz finger fucked the gun over and over, sending shells rolling all over the barbershop.

Lester held up his hands and backed away from the murder scene. "Please, I don't know what they did to you, but I don't have nothin' to do with that. I'm a old man. Please, spare me." He eased beside the pool table. Once there, he hit a switch and a shotgun fell into his hands. He bussed at T.J.

T.J. felt the hot shotgun blast past his face and jumped out of the way. He fell to the floor, bussing at Lester's knees. One of his bullets crashed into Lester's left thigh, buckling him.

"Ahhhhh, you muthafucka!" He hollered. He tried to aim his gun at T.J.

Juelz slipped beside him and placed his gun to his temple. "Windy City shit, nigga."

Boom.

Lester's head opened and coughed up his brain onto the barbershop floor. He lay back with his eyes wide open, struggling to breathe.

T.J. stepped over him with a mug on his face. "Yo li'l bitch ass almost had me. That's funny." He stomped him in the face and emptied his clip before grabbing the duffel bag off of the pool table and rushing from the barbershop.

***

Two days later, Kammron paid both Juelz and T.J, healthy sums of money, and gave them two Bentley trucks as gifts. He promised to use them for further endeavors, and agreed to plug his coke into the city of Chicago as long as they would work for him, annihilating the competition that he had in New York and along the east coast. There were agreements across the board, and on that day, Kammron and Duke Da God plugged into the Born Heartless Animals of Chicago. That's when things really started to take off for the set.

T.J. Edwards

Chapter 9

Kammron stepped in front of the full length mirror and looked himself over. He was fitted in a pink and black Chanel outfit with matching Balenciaga's. He had a million dollars' worth of jewelry around his neck, and another million in pink and white ice on each one of his wrists. His frames were Gucci, and he felt like the boss that he was. Reyanna and Henny took lint rollers and gave his clothes a once over, while Kammron cheesed and ran his tongue across his teeth.

"Shorty, y'all tell me what nigga in the world is more fresher than Kammron? Straight up. If you bitches can name any nigga right now, I'll give both of you hoes a hunnit stacks a piece."

Reyanna had been living with Kammron for two months now. She saw that both he and Henny were strictly about their paper, and slowly she was beginning to become about hers as well. "What about Dame? That nigga be fresh as hell, too. And he be rocking all of that new fashion shit that come from France, and all of that." She stood up and looked into his face.

"You think Dame fresher than me? Really, bitch? I'm sitting here rocking two million dollars' worth of jewelry, and fifteen thousand dollars' worth of clothes. All of my money bred by the slums of Harlem, and you think that nigga got somethin' on me?"

Reyanna swallowed her spit and looked over to Henny for support. "I ain't saying that he got nothing on you, daddy. I'm just sayin'..."

Henny stepped into her face. "You just saying what? That another nigga fuckin' wit daddy? You gotta be out of yo rabid ass mind. Bitch, check yo self."

Reyanna frowned and nudged Henny out of her face. "You trying to twist my words around to mean somethin' that they don't. There ain't a nigga alive that got nothin' on daddy, but when it come to being fly, Dame a give anybody a run for their money."

"Fuck Dame, that nigga ain't risking his life every single day in the slums in order to put that high priced fashion on his back and ours. Word to Harlem, if daddy gave me the word, I'd smoke that punk with no hesitation. Fuck him, and you for making that dumb ass comment." Henny began to shake.

"Whoa, whoa, whoa, ladies." Kammron laughed. "It ain't that serious. Y'all know he can't fuck in my bidness. Can't no nigga do that. But that was a nice try anyway, though, Reyanna." He laughed again. "Bitch, leave the room and let me holler at Henny for a minute."

Reyanna rolled her eyes. She was jealous and angry. She felt like she'd been set up with a trick question. Next time she would allow Henny to answer first, and take her lead. She now understood how the game went. She slipped past Kammron. He snickered.

As soon as she left the room, Kammron closed the door and stepped into Henny's face. He pulled her into his arms. "You love yo mafuckin' daddy, don't you?"

"Hell yeah. In my opinion, ain't nobody got nothin' on you. I'll fry a bitch or a nigga that think anything different. You my fuckin' daddy. That's how I feel, and that's what I'm standing on."

Kammron, kissed her juicy lips that were heavily glossed. He licked them, and looked into her eyes. "You know you my baby girl, right? Like on some real shit, you know I'd blow a nigga over you."

Henny nodded. "I hope that's the truth, although I ain't been feeling like that ever since you allowed for Reyanna to move in. It seems to me like you treat her more like your baby girl than you do me. My li'l heart is hurting."

"What? Man, never that. You the first lady of the Coke Kings. I told you that when I first picked you up. I meant that shit. When a mafucka sees you, they should see the set."

"I'm just telling you how I feel. I don't want you to make me feel stupid for how I feel, daddy." She felt herself becoming emotional and tried to think of angry thoughts so that those vulnerable feelings would go away.

"Well that's my bad, boo. I gotta get better at making you feel better because, even though I don't allow for my emotions to dictate how I feel about a situation, I gotta keep in mind that I'm dealing with a delicate flower."

"I'm ya Earth, daddy. You are my god. That means that you have to protect every element of me at all times. I need you every second of each day. I'll do anything for you because I feel like you do everything for me, except cater to the inner emotional woman that is me, and sometimes that is when I need you the most, daddy. So what can we do about that?"

Kammron sighed and kissed her forehead. He looked into her eyes and shook his head. "Hand to Jehovah, li'l boo, I don't know how to communicate on that soft shit. I am trying, but that shit just ain't in me as much as I wish it was, specifically for you. Nevertheless, you are my li'l mommas, and all I can do is try. How does that sound?"

She shrugged her shoulders. "Sounds good if you actually stand on that. And besides that, this thing with Reyanna is hurting me a little bit. I feel like ever since you allowed her to come to live wit' us, you've been treating her more like yo' baby girl than you do me, and I was here first. That ain't fair, and you know it ain't."

"What? Man, fuck Reyanna, you my mafuckin shorty. I told you when I first knocked yo' ass that your place was to be the first lady of the set. When mafuckas see you, that's the first thing they should think of. If you feel like I've been preferring that li'l bitch over you, it was in your right to say something. Daddy sorry, baby. Cool?"

Henny hated herself for becoming so emotional. "Yes, daddy." She stepped on her tippy toes and kissed Kammron's juicy lips. "I'm sorry for being so whiny."

"It's all good." Kammron kissed her forehead again. "You just love yo' daddy, ain't nothin' wrong wit' that." He eased out of her embrace and handed her the lint roller. "All that hugging and shit done got my shit a li'l out of place. Get me back right."

Henny laughed. "Okay, daddy. I should've known that was coming. But I'ma get you right. You for real what you said about me being first lady to our mafia?"

"You muthafuckin' right. Don't let no bitch impede on your throne. If you ever feel like some shit ain't right, you check it in right away. That's your place."

"Say less." She took her time to get him right. When she finished, Kammron was back fresh and spiffy.

***

Duke Da God adjusted himself in the soft leather seat and pushed his Gucci frames back on his nose. He scanned the first class club through tints, while he sat back, bossed up in Burberry from head to toe. He had a million dollars' worth of jewelry around his neck, and it sparkled in the club every time the lights hit it just right, while he sat in the V.I.P. section that was reserved for top notch bosses, like himself and Kammron.

Kammron came out of his nod and scratched his inner forearm. He was high off of Percocets, Mollie, and two grams of West Indies heroin. "Say, kid, why the fuck am I meeting with this nigga, Dame? What the fuck do he got to offer the

Coke Kings?" Kammron asked, while he scanned the club with his eyes.

There were so many half-dressed dimes there that Duke kept saying "damn" every few minutes. Every time he thought he'd seen the baddest bitch there, somethin' more exotic would walk past and cause him to curse under his breath. "Yo, son, that nigga wanna talk some major bidness wit you. Yo name ringing in the streets and..."

"That nigga bet not be talkin' about trying to sign me for shit. I'm Killa Kam, King of Harlem and the Don of the Coke Kings. I don't work for nobody, mafuckas work for me. I swear, if that nigga get to talking about making me one of his rapping ass employees, I'm smoking him, that's word to Harlem." The mixture of drugs had Kammron flying high, he was easily angered.

Duke drank from his Moët. "N'all, kid, while I did tell him that you had that sauce and stupid word play, Dunn on some other shit. He was fuckin' with that fool Sean, and I guess they had a falling out over some money shit and a bitch. That's just what the internet says. But anyway, he lost a lot of funding and a few rappers and Kid knows that Harlem is the epicenter of New York's talent. He wanna poach some shit, go into bidness wit' Harlem, and in order to do that, he knows he gotta run shit by you. That's the game."

Kammron scratched his thighs, and nodded. "Aiight then, that sound more like it."

Duke looked up and saw Dame and a few members from his crew stop at the velvet ropes outside of Duke and Kammron's V.I.P. section. Duke nodded for their Harlem security to let the man pass, after he was pat down, along with his two bodyguards. Duke stood up and shook his hand. Kammron stayed seated and seemed disinterested, purposely.

Dame stepped over to Kammron and extended his hand. "What's good, god?"

Kammron balled up his fists and held it out to Dame. "Peaceful, let's get right down to bidness. Have a seat."

Dame had a low haircut, and five hundred thousand dollars' worth of ice on his neck. He was short, with a serious face. "Awright, my nigga, you like to get to bidness and I like that. Here's the skinny, I'm looking for a new partner that got a little clout throughout New York. While I could've gone to any other borough and got down with a few other bosses, I'm choosing Harlem. Y'all got rappers on top of rappers that get to it. In addition to that, I wanna help you expand yo' trade of things into the global market. I got plugs all over the world that's guaranteed to increase your profits by three hundred percent. All I'm asking is that you give me the key to Harlem and its talents, and I'll give you what I got. Plus, I heard you get down, too. Ya man's gave me one of yo mixtapes that he put on sound cloud. You live, kid, no cap."

"I already know that. I'll eat a nigga alive like the walking dead, but that's another day. When you say you can help me expand, I take it you mean wit' this coke shit and this West Indies work."

"I know what you do, Kammron, just like you know my work. I know you're sitting on a few million and when you get to this level them bosses gon' come out of the wood work to team up with you, or against you. I'm looking to team up with you for the greater good of Harlem. I'm talking music, movies, everything. Y'all got some bad goddesses in the borough, too. We can even get on some porno shit and strip clubs. The sky's the limit." Dame was dead serious.

"And I fly first class through that bitch. Plus, I'm on my way to getting a private jet, so even the sky ain't the limit no more." Kammron jacked and sipped from his bottle of champagne.

Dame nodded his head. "You fuck wit me and I'll buy that bitch for you as a token of my partnership. I got two of em' and I gotta upgrade sooner or later." He pulled back his suit coat. He was fitted in Roberto Cavili.

Kammron raised his right eyebrow. He knew that Dame had just one upped him, and he didn't like it. But at the same time, he smelled money, along with a prosperous opportunity. He couldn't pass it up. "Say, Dame, I'ma give you the key to my borough, but any nigga you sign gotta be approved by the Coke Kings, and they must pay a fee to the set. That's the way that shit gon' go, so you can structure their contract accordingly. Secondly, I dabble in this rap shit, too, so I'ma put some shit together and use your resources to do my thing. Lastly, when it comes to this dope shit, the split is seventy-five twenty-five. My way. You dig that?"

Dame nodded. "Yeah, it's a go like a green light. Of course, we gon' have to go over some of the logistics, but it's good." He extended his hand again.

Kammron mugged him, and held out his fist. "It's all love."

Dame bumped fists and stood up. "I'll be in touch. Duke Da God, I'm in your debt. Word to Brooklyn."

Duke saluted him and watched as Dame and his crew left out of their section. Duke picked up his bottle of Moët again. "So what you think, Killa?"

"I think we gon' fuck wit Dame for a few months, and then I'ma take over his company and all of his connects. Harlem runs the world, and we don't partner wit' nobody. It's one throne, and that's my seat. I got one right hand, and that's you, Duke. Fuck everybody else. Straight up."

Duke held up his bottle. "To Uptown."

"To North New York." Kammron clunked his bottle, and sipped out of it with devious thoughts roaming through his mind. It was time to chase millions. No longer was he thinking anything less than M's.

***

"You were supposed to check in with me two weeks ago, Kammron. How fuckin' hard is it for you to follow the rules that were assigned to you?" Agent Bishop flicked his cigarette butt over the bridge that overlooked the Hudson River. He frowned at Kammron, and was ready to throw him into the slammer.

Kammron sat on the hood of his Wraith, texting Duke on his cellphone. His platinum Patek watch was flooded with VV's. "Yo', it's hard for me to follow rules, you know that. But chill yo li'l pink ass out. We all good." He finished his message to Duke, telling him that they needed to meet up to discuss shipment pickups of pink fish scale Cocaine from Ponchie out of Washington D.C. "Anyway, I hear you were able to get convictions on those Peter McGuire murders. I saw yo' name being held in the highest esteem in the New York Times, congratulations."

Bishop sighed. "That doesn't have anything to do with your rule violations, Kammron. You can't go about breaking connection from me without getting permission from the FBI. That makes you in breach of your legal contract. If you are found to have broken your terms, and let's say all of these indictments happen tomorrow, by law, you could be indicted right along with everybody else. Our deals will be null and voided."

Kammron stood up and checked his watch. It was one in the morning. "Yo, if you talkin' like you gon' indict the kid, then I'm finna give the government a reason to fuck wit me. I'm Kammron, not John Gotti. That nigga ain't got shit on me. I'm the king of Harlem. Fuck is wrong wit you understanding that?"

"Harlem belongs to America. You're a peasant in the grand scheme of things. Nothing more than a pawn. When Uncle Sam is ready to eat you up and spit you out, you'll be less than mucous on a sidewalk."

Kammron stepped into his face. He had on a Coca-Cola mink. The big diamonds in his ear lobes were the color of Mountain Dew soda pop. "That's what you think?"

"Yeah, that's what I think, Kammron. What you gotta say about that? You're so fuckin' ignorant. You really think you're the king of anything?" He scoffed. "The closest somebody like you ever got to being king was Barack Obama, and I promise you from the bottom of my heart that America and the powers that be will never allow for that to happen again. We'll burn this bitch to the ground first."

"Yeah, muthafucka?" Kammron hissed.

"As long as you dumb fuckers are in your ghettos, or your hoods, killing one another, you will find us supporting you. But the minute you bring that monkey shit out of your sections and into our parts, you will be crushed. You aren't a king. Kings are of white societies, and have European descent. The last time your kind was considered a king, we were bringing you son of bitches over by the boatload just to prove to you that you were less than a true king's animal. Now that's a history lesson for your ass." He bumped Kammron and walked off. "If this happens again, you're going on a thirty day sanction. I'm already considering putting you on a bracelet. I need to sleep on it. Good night, king." He broke up laughing, got into his Nissan, and pulled away from the parking spot.

Kammron stood there watching Agent Bishop's car until it disappeared out of his view, and left him standing there in the darkness. His chest heaved up and down. He clenched and unclenched his jaw. Finally, he hurried to his wraith and got behind the wheel. He turned it on, and stepped on the gas.

Chapter 10

Agent Bishop stepped onto his porch two hours later, after stopping at the local pub and having a few drinks. He placed the key in the lock. He opened the door and closed it behind him. "Honey, I'm home." He loosened his tie and pulled it from around his neck. He was tired, his feet hurt. He kicked off his Italian loafers and stepped further into the dark house. His right hand searched for the light switch. He flipped it on, and his eyes got as big as paper plates.

Kammron stood in the middle of the living room with a big smile on his face. He wore a black beater with a neck full of jewelry. He had a black Mach .11 in his hand. Beside him was Duke. Duke had two shotguns. One was pointed at Agent Bishop's wife's temple, and the other at his daughter's. Duke's face was covered by a red bandana.

Kammron stepped forward. He took a gold crown off of the table and placed it on his head. "Bring yo bitch ass in here and sit the fuck down, after you put that gun on the floor. Now."

Agent Bishop saw the tears coming down his girl's cheeks. He felt horrible. "Kammron, what the fuck is this about?" He asked, unleashing his gun and sliding it across the floor toward Kammron.

Kammron bent down and picked it up. He placed it on his waist. "I'm finna do to yo' women what yo' people did to mine and see how you like it. Bitch, I'ma show you what it feels like to be a true king. Tie 'em up."

Kammron's goons came out of the shadows with duct tape and zip ties. In a matter of minutes, they had Agent Bishop bound and seated on the couch. He shook and tried his best to break the binds, but it was of no use. He hollered into his duct tape.

Kammron bent down in front of Agent Bishop's wife. He rubbed her face. "Check dis out, lady. I'm finna take this duct tape off of you and you ain't gon' scream. Yo' husband is in some real deep shit, and it's in your best interest to not add to it. If you understand me, nod your head."

She nodded.

Kammron removed the duct tape. He ran his hand over her blond hair. "I gotta be honest, I didn't expect for you to be so gorgeous, with these blue eyes, and nice tight body. Bishop, you got a li'l sauce, huh?" Kammron laughed. He looked into her eyes. "You ever been with a Harlem nigga before?"

She shook her head. "No, I've never been with any man other than him. Please don't hurt us." Her bottom lip quivered.

Kammron rubbed her bottom lip with his thumb. "Aw, shorty, I don't give a fuck about what you asking me." He ripped open the front of her gown and her breasts slipped out. The nipples were dark pink and pretty to him. He grabbed a hold of the right one and tweaked the nipple with his tongue. It hardened. He sucked on it and slipped his hand up her dress.

Bishop hollered into his duct tape behind him.

Kammron ignored him. He found Bishop's wife's middle to be dripping wet. He stuffed her panties into her sex lips, before yanking her dress backward on her thighs. He could smell her right away. "Hell yeah, dis bitch ready." He bit into her right thigh and licked up and down it. His fingers entered her pussy slowly at first, and then he was fucking her at full speed with them.

She held her mouth wide open with her head thrown back. Her big breasts jumped up and down and on her frame. The nipples now twice as long as they were before. She bucked into his hand and screeched. Kammron diddled her clitoris. He slammed his fingers faster and faster.

"Uhhhhhhhhh. Stop. Stopppppppppppppp," she screamed, as she threw her head back and came hard. It had been so long since she'd reached her peak with anybody other than herself. And always having been an adrenaline junky, the act within itself was over arousing to her.

Kammron pulled his dripping fingers out and held them out for Bishop to see. "Bitch got some good pussy. I can feel it, but she is too old for me. Yo, Duke, fuck dis bitch, Dunn."

A Harlem shooter came out of the hallway and placed his gun to the back of Bishop's wife's head. Duke threw her thighs on his waist and slid into her at full speed. He proceeded to fuck her with no regard.

"Uh. Uh. Uh. Nooooooo. Uh. Shit. Shit. You black son of a... Shit," she moaned.

Kammron side stepped and knelt down in front of Bishop's daughter. "You look more my speed. Say, Bishop, how old is she? If she too young, I ain't gon' fuck wit her?" Kammron laughed. "Say, shorty, I'm finna take this duct tape off of you, and the same goes for you that went for your mother. If you scream, I'm killing you. You got me?"

She nodded.

"Awright." Kammron snatched the tape off. "First off, how old are you?"

She began to shake. "I'm seventeen. I-I-I just turned seventeen."

Kammron felt a chill go through him. He rubbed her surprisingly thick thigh and squeezed it. "Damn, shorty, I ain't never seen no snow bunny this thick before." Behind him were the sounds of Agent Bishop's wife moaning and groaning. Duke had already cum once in her, now he had her bent over the chair, fucking her from behind, while sweat slid down the side of his face.

"What's your name, li'l girl?" Kammron rubbed all over her thighs.

"A-A-Ashley." She was shaking so bad that the chair was rattling.

Kammron slowly pulled up her skirt until the crotch of her white panties came on display. He sniffed and smiled. When the hem of her skirt was around her thighs. He pulled her knees apart and rubbed her folds through the panties. "Damn, Ashley, yo li'l ass thick all around the board.

Agent Bishop was hollering at the top of his lungs into the duct tape. He tried to jump up more than once but Kammron's hittas from Harlem kept him trapped.

Kammron slowly eased her panties down her thighs and off of her slender ankles. Her pink pussy was bald. The lips were plump and slightly separated. He could see the hood of her clitoris peeking outside of her gap. He rubbed it, and rolled his thumb around it over and over until she jerked forward with her mouth wide open. Kammron slid his middle finger into her and felt her blazing heat.

Ashley shivered. "Unnnnh!"

Kammron stood up and pulled his dick out. He pumped it in her face. "Ashley, you ever been with a black nigga before?"

She shook her head. "N-n-no, never. Nobody period, my father won't let me."

Kammron put his dick on her lips. "Suck this, baby. It's okay. Yo father can't tell you shit right now. I'm daddy. Open up."

Ashley opened her mouth and allowed for Kammron to slide past her lips. His dark penis looked super black sliding into her small pink lips. She sucked the head and pulled her face back. Looked past him and to Bishop who was crying tears of anguish. She swallowed the lump in her throat, and closed her eyes. She sucked Kammron back into her mouth and proceeded to give him the best head that she could manage, while he pulled down the straps of her shirt and played with her hard nipples, one by one.

Duke sucked his middle finger and slipped it into Bishop's wife's rosebud over and over, before he spit directly on it and slipped into it with two hard thrusts. "Shit, bitch."

"Uhhh, yes. I mean, no. Stop. Stop. Stop. Stop. Uhhhhhh, fuck, stop." She slammed back into him with her big breasts swinging back and forth on her chest. Duke grabbed her hair and forced her to arch her back while he fucked her at full speed.

Kammron laid Ashley on the floor and got between her thighs. He sucked her neck and lined his dick up. With one thrust of his hips, he sank ten inches deep inside of her virgin pussy. He rolled his hips over and over, plunging deeply. Her ankles wrapped around his waist. "Call me daddy, li'l bitch. Say it." He pounded harder.

"Uh. Uh. Uh. Daddy. Daddy. Unnnnnnn. Daddy," Ashley moaned loudly.

Kammron sucked her hard nipples while he held her breasts together, fucking her like a savage. He leaned down into her ear. "You gon' be my li'l bitch, Ashley. Fuck yo' father. You like this shit, bitch, don't you? Tell the truth." He pushed her knees to her chest and fucked her at full speed while she came and squirted all over his thrusting dick. Her juices leaked out of her and into her ass. Kammron laid back flat and sucked her neck. "Bitch, say you love it."

"I love it," she whispered. "I love it." She felt him deep in the lower region of her stomach. It felt good. She hated herself for getting off to it, but something about their skin had always intrigued her. Agent Bishop had raised her to hate people of color, but she never did. He'd told her that they were forbidden, and that he would disown her if she ever brought one home. The more he forced her to follow his ideology, the more she craved them.

Kammron flipped her over and brought her up to all fours. He fucked her hard, looking Bishop in the eye. "This my baby, now. My li'l bitch. Her pussy good, too. Good and pink." He watched his dick go in and out of her. He trembled. He forced her face into the carpet and came deep inside of her womb with squirt after squirt. Ashley fell on her stomach and Kammron fell on top of her continuing to fuck her at full speed. He pulled out and came all over her ass cheeks some more. Then he sawed his dick up and in between them.

Duke pulled out of Agent Bishop's wife and kissed her on the mouth. "This bitch cold." He stood up and pulled up his pants.

Bishop's wife curled into a ball. She was exhausted. Her pussy continued to quiver. She ran her tongue all over her lips, and moaned deep within her throat.

***

Kammron pushed the shotgun further down Agent Bishop's throat. He gagged over the barrel, while looking up at Kammron from his knees. "Listen to me, Bishop. From here on out, you gon' play by my rules, or your family will be slaughtered in such a way. I don't give a fuck if you turn snake and you try and go to the authorities about tonight. There is no way that they will be able to prevent what's going to happen to you and them, so it's in your best interest to follow behind me. Do I make myself clear?" Kammron pushed the shotgun further down his throat.

Bishop gagged and threw up over the barrel. He pulled his mouth off of it. "Yes, Kammron, I swear to God. Please, just leave. We have an understanding."

"Duke, show dis mafucka what else we got," Kammron ordered, placing the barrel of the shotgun to Bishop's left eye, forcing him to close it.

Duke leaned down and showed Bishop the names and addresses of all of his closest of kin, including his other children that were away at college. It was all courtesy of Kamina. "You try us, and we wipe out ya last name, word to Harlem, and it's King Killa Kam himself."

"Yeah, how you love that?" Kammron smiled. He grabbed Ashley and kissed her lips. "Later, snow baby."

He looked back at Duke. "Let's get the fuck out of here, kid. Mission accomplished." He pulled the long barrel out of Bishop's mouth and they left.

T.J. Edwards

Chapter 11

With Agent Bishop forced to be completely on board from fear for the welfare of his family, Kammron was able to go ten times harder than he did before Agent Bishop ever became a part of his life. Because Bishop was so well connected at the FBI, he was able to give Kammron intelligence on other street crews that were holding large quantities of narcotics all around New York City. Kammron was given blueprints for their operations and their other connects. He learned other crews' habits and shipment patterns. And because he did, he was able to catch them slipping and capitalize off of their misfortunes.

He put together a hit squad and a team of jack boys, whose sole missions were to annihilate other crews, rob them blind, and then bring all of the proceeds back to his throne in Harlem. Once there, Kammron would put all of the spoils up into his store houses, which were guarded by his trusted security savages, who had pledged their allegiances to him, and him only.

Every Friday, Kammron, would pay the workers in his outfit. He paid them according to the amount of work that they put in, the number of bodies they'd dropped during the week, and how much money they brought him from each major shipment of narcotics that he dropped off to their traps. He paid the runners, and the dope boys that operated off of their phones. The only stipulation was that they had to be from Harlem.

In a matter of six months, Kammron built up young savages that were Killa Kam crazy. They honored him as their true king, and most would lay their lives down on the line for him and the set.

Kammron rolled through Harlem with two armed cars in front of whatever extravagant whip he was driving at the moment, and two armed cars in back of him. When he stepped out, he strolled through with no less than ten body guards, whose only job was to murder anything or anybody that looked like a threat to Kammron.

Because Kammron had so much security and was making so much money, with an FBI agent on his team, he saturated himself in millions of dollars' worth of jewelry at a time. His diamonds were all colors of the rainbow. His clothes were just as bright. He took to rocking pinks, yellows, light blues, reds of all kinds, anything that would make him stand out from the rest of the drug lords of New York City. He was Harlem crazy, and a Harlem separatist. He didn't screw with other boroughs. He only had love for his and the men and women that came from the mud of his trenches.

A year after Agent Bishop agreed to come aboard with Kammron, Duke Da God rolled up on Kammron one night while they were visiting Miami. Duke was rolling a fire red Hellcat, fresh off of the lot. It was mid-summer, and hot and humid. Duke jumped out of his whip with two Brazilian twins, one under each of his arms. His neck was so wet with diamonds that he looked like a walking target. He kept five armed security guards with him at all times. None were older than eighteen, and they were all bred in the Harlem River Houses. Duke walked up to Kammron, who was standing on the side of his white Lamborghini with Henny in front of him, and waved for him to step aside so he could holler at him.

Kammron sucked on Henny's neck. "Hold on, boo, let me fuck wit kid real quick."

Henny nodded. "Cool, daddy. I'ma check my makeup in the mirror to make sure that I'm properly representing you."

Henny pulled up the Lamborghini doors, and sat back in the car, while their security remained on high alert.

Kammron walked over to Duke. "What's good?" He was high and breezy off of two Percocets and a gram of some Vietnam heroin Ponchie had hooked them up with.

"Yo, our wolves just put a few of the crews from Queens on the menu. If we approve this move, we are looking to seize at least a million dollars in dope, and a million in cash. We can also stop the flow of goods coming from up that way, so we'll be able to send some of our travelers up there to fill in the blanks of what those niggas won't be able to fill."

"Fuck, is we even discussing this? Pull the trigger. Make that shit happen. Now." Kammron got ready to walk off.

"Kammron, it's not that simple. The crews that our troops are talking about crushing belong to Bonkers. If we unleash them, that nigga about to be poor as hell." Duke stepped up to Kammron. "You sho you wanna do that?"

Kammron lowered his head and rubbed the hairs on his chin. He had a Yankees fitted barely on the top of his head so his deep waves could be seen. It was slightly tilted to the left. "Yo, that nigga out there getting M's like that wit dem Queens niggas?"

"Apparently. Word through the pack is that he is making close to a hundred thousand dollars a week. He really moving hard out in Jamaica, Queens." Duke sparked his blunt. Thoughts of Deanna crossed his mind. He tried to block them out.

"Yo', if he's getting money out there in Queens, that means he turned his back on Harlem. Anybody that ain't rollin' wit Harlem is rolling against it. I love that nigga, but I love my borough more. If his niggas are on the menu, then eat 'em like they the main course. Spare Bonkers, though. Give him a chance to kiss the ring."

Duke Da God nodded. "Awright, we'll jump on that shit wit dem niggas first thing in the wee hours of tonight." Duke puffed off of his blunt and blew the smoke in the air. "I know this might not be the best time to bring this topic up, but what about Deanna, man? I've been missing my seed."

Kammron smiled. "Oh, I ain't tell you? I found her, and contrary to what you was thinking, she was safe and sound. I had Henny do some digging and it turns out that Jason's bitch ass had a baby mother who was scorned by him. Her name is Vett. She gave Deanna to Henny, and Henny took her straight to the hospital to make sure that she wasn't touched or nothing like that. Thank Jehovah that she wasn't. Long story short, yo birthday tomorrow and us delivering her to you safe and sound was going to be your gift."

Duke looked into Kammron's eyes. "You shitting me, Killa?"

"I don't even play video games."

Duke froze, and then hugged Kammron. "Nig-ga!" He tried to pick him up.

Kammron wiggled out of his embrace and pushed him back. He straightened his clothes and adjusted his jewelry. "Come on, Dunn, you making a boss look fucked up in public. You welcome."

Duke nodded. "Damn, Kammron. I love yo ass. Yo, word to Deanna, I love you." He thought about hugging him again and decided against it.

Henny stepped out of the Lamborghini that was so low she had to squat to get out of it. "Damn, Killa, you told him the surprise already?"

Duke Da God rushed to pick her up. "Come here."

Henny sidestepped him and held her arms straight out. "Yo, don't no nigga touch the first lady, other than Killa. Duke, you elated. That's good, but back ya ass up and give me my space." She balled her fist as best she could with her manicured nails.

Duke stopped and laughed. "Man, fuck y'all. Killa, I'm finna handle dis bidness and then I wanna see my baby. I need a week to spend with her. I ain't accepting no for an answer."

"I'll think about it. Just make that other shit happen tonight. Word up." Kammron rubbed his hands together anxiously before Henny stepped in front of him with her lip gloss shining. He opened his arms for her. She turned her back and eased into his embrace, laying against his chest. "You missing daddy?"

"Yeah, I love when you hold me. Can't nobody do me like you, Killa." She rubbed her ass into his lap.

"Yo, and a mafucka ain't even finna get the opportunity to try. This pussy belongs to the king, ain't that right?"

"You muthafuckin' right." She smiled, and closed her eyes, relishing the feeling of being held by Harlem's great.

***

Kammron's stomach rumbled. He burped and held his fist in front of his mouth. Henny, looked up at him. He mugged her. "Yo, the kid gotta hit up this casino bathroom. My stomach fuckin' wit me again. Chill here, I'll be back." He made haste to the restroom, and straight for the last stall. After grabbing the hand sanitizer off of the counter of the lavatory, and using it to clean up his stall, he covered the entire seat with tissue and sat down, releasing his bowels.

The door swung open and closed back loudly. Kammron heard the sounds of footsteps and then they stopped. The door opened again and in walked another person. The footsteps were equally loud and then they stopped.

"Ahmad says it has to be tonight. I got the poison. You put it in his drink, and we are all rich men. Besides, he's the only one that doesn't want to venture off in the narcotics trade. You gotta get with the times, man, or our family is going to be left in the dust. All of the Islamic families are wetting their whistle this way. As long as we stay away from the usage of it, we're in law. He's being an extremist. We'll prosper further with Ahmad at the head. He should've been seated on the throne next anyway, if it wasn't for that scandal. Politics suck. But trust me, have I ever steered you wrong?" Sayeed asked, looking into Khalid's eyes.

Khalid sighed and shook his head. "Awright, fuck it. Give me the poison, and let's get it over with."

Kammron got up and peeked his head over the stall. He saw two Arab men, face to face, exchanging the poison that they spoke of. He found them peculiar. He climbed back down and continued to listen.

"Khabir should be getting up to use the bathroom when we get back to the table. You distract him, and I'll pour the mix into his White Russian. The mix will affect his heart in sixty seconds. He'll go into cardiac arrest, and the rest is history. Let's do this." Sayeed hugged Khalid. Both men left the bathroom.

Kammron finished his business and flushed the toilet. He was washing his hands when Khabir came into the bathroom and stepped in front of the middle stall. Khabir, looked over his shoulder at him and bowed his head respectfully. He unzipped his pants and proceeded to piss.

Kammron looked over to the door and expected one of the men from before to come through it. When they didn't, he sized the Arab up quickly. Khabir was five feet five inches tall with thick black hair, and arched eyebrows. He wore a gray and black Versace suit over Versace loafers. His side burns were thin, he was without facial hair. Kammron waited for the man to come to the sink and wash his hands. He side eyed him. "Say, Dunn, you must be one of those rich Arab mafuckas, huh?"

Khabir raised his right eyebrow. "Excuse me?"

Kammron eyed the subtle platinum rings on his fingers and the flamboyant three carat rocks in his ears. "The reason why I ask you is because just a few minutes ago, there were a couple cats here talking about assassinating you to get you out of the way. They say you're stopping the family from venturing off into narcotics and you're being an Islamic extremist."

Khabir took a deep breath and kept his hands under the water, although washing them was the furthest thing from his mind. "Who are you, and what are you talking about?"

"My name is Killa Kam. I'm the king of Harlem, and I thought I might pull ya coat because as of right now, they are adding some kind of poison to your drink that is designed to make your heart stop beating."

"Who is doing this?" Khabir became furious.

"Mafucka, I don't know their names. But they are trying to get you out of the way so Ahmad can take over the family."

"Ahmad is my brother. He squandered his inheritance. I am the Prince that was crowned king of my Saudi royal family after my father died a month ago. Why would they try and do such a thing? I am a fair man."

Kammron dusted off his fit, and fixed his eye brows in the mirror. "I don't know, but you bet not go back out there and drink that White Russian."

As soon as Kammron said the name of the drink that Khabir had been sipping on, Khabir felt like he couldn't breathe. He stumbled sideways and bumped into Kammron.

Kammron held him up. He led him to a stall and sat him on the toilet. He fanned his face.

Khabir shook his head. "I'm trapped. If what you say is true, then they brought me here to Miami to assassinate me. I need to get out of here. Will you help me?"

"Man, I don't know what the fuck you got going on. That shit ain't my bidness. My business is in Harlem."

"I am worth three billion dollars. If you help me, you will never have to work again a day in your life. The world will become your playground."

Kammron switched his tune. "Man, I wasn't about to let them get over on you anyway. I got you. Let me make a phone call and I'ma help you escape this situation. You're worth three billion dollars, though?"

"That's being modest. These men will pay for this treachery. That I can assure you."

"I bet." Kammron walked to the end of the bathroom and called Duke Da God.

Chapter 12

Khabir sat at the table and exhaled. "Whew. Those shrimp did not sit right with me. Thank God, I got them out of my system, though. Anyway, what did I miss?"

Khalid drank from his white wine. "I was just telling Sayeed and Sarah here that after we expand our fuel companies into Dubai this summer, all of our profit margins will rise by thirty percent. Things are sure to take off then. Next, it'll be time to invest in some clean energy technology. That's the new wave."

Khabir nodded. "Yeah, have any of you spoken with Ahmad lately?"

The trio exchanged looks at each other caught off guard.

Sayeed was a heavy set man with big ears and an unattractive face. "You know we're forbidden to speak with him without getting approval from you first? Why would you ask such a question?"

"Just wondering. I know that Ahmad was so beloved by all of the people that saw us rise from poverty. He kept his gutter-like ways, and the boring me chose to transform with the Qur'an as my guide. Silly me." Khabir felt himself becoming heated.

The trio exchanged glances at each other again.

Khalid took the half glass of White Russian infused with poison and slid it across the table. "Boss, I can tell the jet lag is kicking your tail. Here, have a drink. It's your favorite." He side eyed Sarah.

Khabir picked it up and slowly brought it to his lips. Everybody at the table prepared for him to drink the death liquid. They leaned forward toward him when he stopped. He sat the glass down. "Damn it, I left my watch on the counter in the bathroom. Sayeed be a friend and retrieve it for me, will you?"

"Sure Boss." Sayeed removed himself from the table and kept looking over his shoulder to see if Khabir had taken a sip of the poison yet.

When he reached the bathroom, he pushed on the door and stepped inside. He was irritated. "Just drink the fuckin' poison, Khabir, fuck, drink it and we'll all be billionaires in a few years." He rolled his eyes and searched the sink's counter. He saw the Rolex at the end of it. He walked over and got ready to grab it when Kammron came out of the bathroom stall. He walked toward Sayeed. Sayeed ignored him.

Kammron walked right up to Sayeed and slapped his hand on his shoulder. "Yo bitch ass is gon' be one of the three mafuckas that help me to cement my status as one of the greats? Nall, fuck that, not one, THE GREATEST."

Sayeed went to knock Kammron's hand off of him. "Get the fuck off of me, you disgusting ni..."

Duke Da God appeared from the bathroom stall. He slipped the wire around Sayeed's neck three times and pulled him toward the back of the bathroom, where he proceeded to choke him to death while Sayeed fought, scratching and clawing.

Kammron went into the stall and stomped Sayeed with all of his might in the chest, crushing his rib cage. Seconds later, Sayeed was lifeless.

***

"So that will be the most cost effective way for us to make as much money in the European sector as we can. That, I think, deserves a toast, and I am trying my best to wait for Sayeed to get back before we do. Khalid, go and see what's taking him so long. Hurry up. I'm getting restless and I need to recuperate."

"As you wish, boss." Khalid got up from the table and headed to the bathroom. He frowned as soon as Khabir was unable to see his face. "Fuck, he's so exhausting."

Khabir glanced across the table at Sarah. "How is your night going?"

Sarah flipped her silky black hair over her shoulders. "I'm fine, Khabir. Ready to turn in like you, so tomorrow we can grace the beaches. I hear Miami's beaches are second to none."

"You are my niece, correct? You love me?"

Sarah frowned. "Of course, I love you, Khabir. You have been nothing but good to me."

"And do you think I am taking the family in the right direction?"

"That's not for me to debate. I think that you live by the holy book and it is your guide. I have no problem with that."

"And do you think that the family would look better financially if Ahmad was running the show?"

She sipped from her wine and avoided eye contact with him. "Once again, that's not for me to debate."

Khabir lowered his eyes. "Well, thank you for being honest. Hey, just because I can always depend on you to tell me the truth, why don't you take a drink from the king's cup?" He slid his White Russian over to her.

Sarah jumped back. "No, thank you. I have never liked White Russian." She eyed the glass as if it were a plague.

So she does know. Khabir felt his heart break in two. "Okay, honey." He sat back trying his best to remain calm. "They need to hurry up. I am ready to go."

***

Khalid walked up to the bathroom door and saw that there were two big black men standing on the side of it. They eyed him closely, and looked off. He stepped inside of it and the door closed behind him. Kammron was standing at the sink washing his hands. Khalid mugged him. He walked further inside. "Sayeed! Sayeed! Are you here using the Loo?" Loo was another word for bathroom. They used this terminology out in Europe.

Kammron dried his hand on a towel and made it seem as if he was about to leave the bathroom. But when he got close to Khalid, he came from under his shirt and slammed a taser to his throat. He turned it up as high as it could go and dropped him. As soon as he hit the floor, Duke Da God came out of the stall and choked him out, just as he had Sayeed. He pulled him to the end stall that was below the bathroom window.

Kammron opened the door and ordered his goons to do the same thing to Khalid that they'd done to Sayeed. The massive men came inside and hoisted Khalid's dead body up and out of the bathroom window. Once outside, his body was slammed into a trunk, alongside Sayeed, and the hittas from Harlem pulled off with him.

***

Kammron walked up to the table and stopped. "Yo, I think you left this watch in the bathroom. I just wanted to return it." He set it on the table and walked off with the sounds of his chains knocking into each other. Khabir took his watch and smiled. "Well that was nice of him. But where are they? Go and tell them to come on," he snapped.

Sarah removed herself from the table and rushed into the men's bathroom. When she got there, they were nowhere to be found. She came and reported that back to Khabir.

"Fuck it, let's go. Finish your drink." He took his and swallowed it in three gulps.

Sarah bucked her eyes. She grabbed her wine and finished it. She stopped for a second and beat on her chest. "That's strong, it tastes mixed with somethin'."

Khabir sat back down and looked up at her. "Well silly me, I think we might've got our drinks mixed up."

Sarah took a step back. "You knew?" She was fearful. "But you didn't."

"An eye for an eye." Khabir snickered.

Sarah felt her heart start to beat faster and faster. Her throat began to tighten. Her lungs contracted and then started to expand further and further apart.

"Khabir, how could you?" Her voice was raspy. Her heart beat a hundred times and then once really hard before it exploded. She shook and fell to her knees. Blood traveled up her throat and came out of her mouth and nose. She blinked and tried to reach out for Khabir. Her insides twisted. She spit out a piece of her heart and then she was dead.

***

Three days later, Kammron strolled into Khabir's Manhattan office with Duke Da God beside him. Before he took a seat, he placed two mayonnaise jars on the table before Khabir. Both jars were filled with Sayeed and Khalid's parts. One had both of their tongues, and the other had their hearts stuffed inside of it.

Khabir took one look at them and smiled. "I like you, Kammron. You are what I have needed on my team."

"I'm what every mafucka needs on their team. Let's talk dividends." Kammron sat back and kicked his Timbs up on Khabir's desk. "How are you going to make shit make sense for the Coke Kings?"

Khabir snapped his fingers. The double doors to his office opened and in walked two beautiful Arab women. One held two suitcases and the other two duffel bags. They sat them on the side of Kammron and walked out with their asses jiggling in their skirts. Kammron shook his head. They looked perfect.

"This is a gift and a token of my appreciation. Four million dollars. You can do whatever you want with it." Khabir assured him.

Kammron perked up. "Yo it's two million in each bag?"

Khabir nodded. "Yes."

Kammron picked up a duffel and placed it on Duke's lap. "Love, fool."

Duke unzipped the bag and looked over the crisp bills. "Love, nigga, damn."

Kammron looked over to Khabir. "This it?"

"Of course not." He nodded toward the suitcase.

Kammron grabbed one of them and popped it open. Inside were twenty kilos of Israeli heroin. The packages had Arabic written all over them. Kammron picked them up. "What's this shit?"

"That is pure Israeli heroin, fresh from the fields. You will find none stronger, or worth more than this. Street value sixty thousand a kilo."

Kammron closed the suitcase back and handed it to Duke Da God. "Both of these suitcases are going to my right hand. Dawg, I know this ain't it. I feel like you baby mama-ing me."

"What do you mean, Kammron? I don't understand." Khabir sat up.

"You are worth three billion? You throwing peanuts at me, kid. I don't like that shit. I saved your life by using my crew. Therefore you owe me some serious dough. Stop trying to spoon feed me, nigga. That shit ain't one hunnit." Kammron was ready to slap him from across the desk.

"You can always tell the nature of a man by the way he accepts gifts." Khabir sat back and crossed his legs.

"Oh yeah, and what does my nature say?" Kammron sat on the edge of his chair, ready to pounce. Duke peeped his body language and got prepared.

"It says that you are a man of prestige and quality. That you refuse to accept less than what you deserve. You are fair but pig-headed." Khabir smiled "And I like that. What do you think you should receive?"

"A Billi." Kammron's eyes grew into slits.

Khabir nodded. "As you would." He was quiet. He rolled his chair back and got to texting away on his lap top. He pulled up images of Harlem on his computer. "You are from Harlem, New York. Am I right?"

"Black heaven, you muthafuckin' right." Kammron, rubber necked to look at the images on his computer.

"Harlem is struggling with poverty, worse now than it did during the great depression. Many families are barely at the poverty line, and they are close to facing gentrification. Let's say we do something for Harlem that no other borough will be able to say happened for them."

Kammron stood up. "Oh yeah, and what's that?"

"Kammron when I am done with your borough, you will be proud to call yourself the king of it."

T.J. Edwards

Chapter 13

While Khabir was fulfilling his promises to rebuild Harlem from the ground up, Kammron's crew of lethal savages went on a rampage, dismantling and destroying every trap house and dope boy that posed a serious threat to Harlem and Kammron's operations. They kicked in doors, and had no problem with slaying every person inside, after emptying the trap house of its goods. All of the merchandise was brought before Duke Da God. He sifted through the spoils and placed the things that were useful inside of Kammron's vault. Then he would send his troops back into the field for days at a time.

A week after the raids began, Khabir supplied Kammron with three hundred AK47s, a military issue. Kammron handed them out to his troops, and the city of New York's murder rate rose by twenty percent. They over killed and made examples out of the hustlers in Queens.

While his killas were over in Queens causing mayhem, Kammron flooded Harlem with the Israeli heroin, and left it so pure that until he got the perfect balance right, citizens of Harlem were dying left and right from overdoses. Kammron went into the kitchen with Duke Da God and whipped up the perfect batch and released it back onto the streets. While a few overdosed Tue rate of doing so curved dramatically. He decided to serve his addicts his product at seventy five percent, giving them room to step on the work themselves.

In a matter of two months, Harlem was hip to the Israeli heroin and hooked. Kammron's profits shot up by three hundred percent.

Duke Da God hired more workers. He drafted them fresh out of middle school. He gave them packs and made sure that the set paid all of their parents' bills and supplied them with weekly groceries. The young hustlers were paid in clothes and jewelry. Money rarely touched their hands, leaving them dependent.

Kammron knew it was imperative to always leave his workers dependent on him. So he gave them the things that they asked for, but he never put money in their hands. Money equaled power. He wanted to maintain the power. To maintain the power, he needed to control the dollar flow in and out of Harlem, and that's what he did.

Khabir dumped three hundred kilos of Israeli product on him once every two weeks. Because the product was coming so often, and eighty percent of it was pure profit, Kammron, thought it was smart to venture off into Queens. His troops had already ransacked the borough, using murder as a weapon. The borough was weak and in need of a true King. Kammron wanted to be that king. He would take over a portion of the borough and rename it, Harlem.

A week before he was set to put this plan in motion, he received word from Bonkers. He wanted to meet up. The matter was supposed to be serious.

It was eleven o'clock on a hot summer night when Kammron stepped out of his black on black Hummer with the all red leather interior, dressed in Gucci fatigues and black Gucci Military boots. Beside him was Duke Da God, and behind them were fifty troops from Harlem. All were in fatigues and armed to the fullest with assault rifles and handguns. Kammron had a Kevlar vest over his chest and three million dollars' worth of jewelry around his neck. Kammron looked over the Pier and adjusted the .40 caliber in his waistband as the rocks of the parking lot crunched under his boots.

Bonkers stepped out of his Range Rover with a cellphone to his ear and a big blunt in his mouth. He hung up the phone. In the dark parking lot behind him were twenty of his Queens killas. Half of their faces were covered with black bandanas. They were armed and ready to go to war over Bonkers, if need be. Bonkers extended his hand to Kammron.

Kammron shook it and pulled Bonkers into his embrace. He hugged him. "Long time no see, kid, word up."

"Long time no see, Killa. I wish I was calling you here for a better reason, but this is what it is." He walked off and Kammron followed him. When Bonkers felt they were out of the earshot of the troops, Bonkers spoke up. "I gotta crush Jimmy."

Kammron was quiet for a moment. He nodded. "Awright, what else?"

"Yo', Kid has been trying to dismantle me from the inside out. He set me up with a little turf out in Queens and supplied me with a little work. Ever since then, my shit been getting hit left and right. The niggas who been doing it know my operations inside and out. My drop off dates. My pickups. Who my runners are. My shooters. I know it's Jimmy, and that ain't it." Bonkers lowered his head. "Yo, that bitch Yasmin been foul all along. After that shit took place with you and her while I was down, I had my suspicions, so I went and got a DNA test for Yasmin and Coke. Turns out that ain't neither one of those kids mine. Yazzy belongs to Jimmy, and I'm guessing that Coke belongs to you."

"Damn, son, word up?" Kammron placed his hand on his shoulder.

"Word up." Bonkers felt himself trembling.

"Yo', I can apologize a million times but that ain't gon' do shit. I got mad love for you, and that shit will never change. What do you need for me to do?" Kammron looked over his shoulder and saw that his troops were lined up behind him with assault rifles in their hands.

113

"If I do wind up going at Jimmy, and killing him, those mafuckas from Jamaica gon' be at my head like a skull cap. I need to know that I can depend on Harlem to have my back."

Kammron frowned. "I am Harlem, nigga. Yo, you do what you gotta do, and let me know when you need me. Until then, I got some shit I need to drop in yo' lap."

"Gon' head." Bonkers looked him over.

"You already know how fast words make it around the Apple. Turns out that the talk done got back to Harlem. They say that Queens ain't got a steady supplier no more, and the borough is broken. I need a few territories in that bitch. I wanna open up a shop on at least fifty blocks, call that bitch Baby Harlem, with your blessing of course." Kammron curled his upper lip.

Bonkers nodded. "You hold me down with this war against Jimmy, and those blocks at yours. I'm thinking about growth and expansion toward Brooklyn anyway. Most Queens niggas ain't loyal. The only problem is those Vega Boys. Word is that they are handling business out in China right now, and when they get back, they are coming for Brooklyn again. I wanna sew up the Red Hook Projects and everything surrounding that bitch. But first things first, I gotta crush my own brother. This shit about to be hard for me."

"I'm yo mafuckin' brother, nigga. Fuck Jimmy. Do what you gotta do." Kammron placed his hand on his shoulder. "It's all about chasing a Billi. Fuck M's. That's baby money. Crush that nigga and get rich. Harlem gon' watch from a distance, but we're here."

Bonkers hugged him. "Did you know that Jimmy was fuckin' Yasmin behind my back?"

"Wait, that ain't what this is all about, is it?" Kammron wanted to make sure before he involved his borough. Harlem didn't give a fuck about quarrels over pussy. Kammron felt like Harlem had the best goddesses in all of the world.

"Nah, kid, it's deeper than that. But I'd be lying if I said that it didn't have its place in my heart. Love is a crash thing. Nevertheless, business is business. I love you, Dunn. I'm finna chase my legacy. Word up."

They shook up once again. Kammron returned Bonkers' love, then both sides disappeared and went their separate ways.

***

A week later, while Kammron was strategically moving his Harlem units into Queens, Bonkers called a one on one sit down with Jimmy the Capo. They met up at Jimmy's estate out in the Hamptons. Bonkers stepped out of his Range Rover and walked up to the three story mansion, knocking on the door. He waited a full minute before Jimmy opened the door with a smile on his face.

"What it do, God?" Bonkers grabbed his brother and gave him a half hug.

Jimmy hugged him back. "Come on in, kid."

Bonkers walked into the mansion and looked around. The statues and expensive paintings always flattered him. Even though his brother was a slum raised Harlem nigga, like him, he had exotic taste. Bonkers didn't know where it came from. "I appreciate you for fuckin' wit me so swiftly. That shit means a lot to me."

"Man, stop playin'. You my li'l brother. Why wouldn't I make time for you?" Jimmy led him through the house until they got into his media room. Once there, he took a seat. "So what's good?"

Bonkers sat across the table from him. "Yo, I don't wanna get lost to far on this whole Yasmin thing, but the fact that Yazzy is yours is really fuckin' wit my head. How long have you known?"

Jimmy shrugged his shoulders. "I don't know. What I can say is that a bitch is always gon' fuck with the nigga she know got the most money and pull, especially hoes from the ghetto. I fucked a few times, and she became old news. You fell for her, so I kept that secret to myself. Who was I to break up y'all happy home?"

"But you got her pregnant, and you let me play step daddy to your seed. The whole time you were laughing at me."

Jimmy snickered. "Kid, you spacing. I never did that. I fucked. I didn't think shit of it. Anyway, time is money, I ain't finna sit here and talk about a bitch. Fuck her. What else you wanna talk about?" Jimmy picked up his platter of Colombian cocaine and tooted two lines. He sat it back down as the beats of his heart began to pound.

"Queens."

"Yeah, about that. It seems like ever since you been running shit out there, the profits have fallen off by eighty percent. We are hemorrhaging both money and dope. I think I gotta remove you from your post, effective immediately." Jimmy kicked back and pulled his nose. "The Byrd Gang will handle that borough from here on out. Maybe you should think of Staten Island or

somethin' light. Brooklyn locked down, so is Harlem, for now, until I come for it." He laughed.

"You think I'm some li'l weak ass nigga, huh?" Bonkers felt his adrenalin surging through him.

"Nah, kid, I think that you just ain't got that boss shit in you like that. Everybody can't be a Don, some niggas gotta be the workers." Jimmy stood up and opened his liquor cabinet.

He turned his back on Bonkers and poured himself a glass of Scotch. "Maybe you should fall under Kammron. As much as I don't like that nigga, he got that boss shit in him. I know he'd make sure you're straight at all times. Or I don't know what to tell you." He turned around and dropped his glass of liquor.

Bonkers had two .44 silenced Desert Eagles aimed at him. "Bitch nigga, I'm finna be the king of New York. I don't give a fuck if you believe in me or not. Fuck you. Fuck Yasmin, and fuck Kammron. It's only me. Am I my brother's keeper?"

"But, Bonkers, I was just bullshitting. You know I love..."

"Man, fuck you." Bonkers pulled the triggers over and over, spitting bullet after bullet into Jimmy.

The slugs carried Jimmy into his liquor cabinet. Glass splashed everywhere. Bonkers continued to shoot him, over and over, until he fell on the ground and curled into a ball. Bonkers fired more slugs. "I'm the king. I'm the king. Fuck you, Jimmy. Fuck you and fuck Kammron. Die. Die. Die," Bonkers said through gritted teeth as he emptied his clips.

Immediately, he got his thoughts in order, wrapped Jimmy in a rug, and loaded him into the trunk of his car, with the intention of dropping him in the Hudson River already on his mind as he made haste from Jimmy's mansion.

***

When Bonkers made it back home, Yasmin had her suitcases packed at the door of their home. Her face was tear streaked. She hadn't eaten in two days, ever since the truth had come out about both Yazzy and Coke. She didn't even look up at Bonkers as he came into the house.

Yazzy sat on the couch with her head down. She was also sad after hearing the news that Bonkers wasn't her daddy. She got up from the couch and ran to Bonkers, expecting him to pick her up.

Bonkers ignored her, even when she began to jump up and down, crying. "Where are you going?" He asked Yasmin.

"North Carolina. I can't take Harlem no more." She brushed past him. "You can't see that girl crying out for you?"

Bonkers lowered his head and shook it. "Damn, why shit have to be like this? Why did you have to be such a hoe?"

Yasmin stopped in her tracks. "Don't use that kind of language in front of my daughter. That ain't right, Bonkers. It ain't and you know it." She began to cry. "I loved you."

"Shut up, bitch. Stop lying so much. Shut up," he snapped.

"Stop fighting. Please stop it!" Yazzy covered her ears.

Bonkers shook his head. With blazing speed, he grabbed Yazzy by the throat and picked her up in the air, choking her with all of his might. He slammed her head against the corner of the doorway and snapped her neck. A bone stuck through it. He kept choking.

"No. No. Stop," Yasmin screamed as she jumped on his back.

Bonkers choked Yazzy until he killed her. Then he slung Yasmin off of his back and straddled her. He punched her in the face, over and over, as hard as he could. His knuckles broke her facial bones and shattered her eye sockets. He kept punching and punching.

"You dogged me. You stabbed me in the back. Die. Die. Die." He choked her neck while she kicked her feet until her eyes crossed and she passed away. Then he stood up, looking down on her. "They all gon' feel my wrath. All of them. I'm the king."

He dragged both Yazzy and Yasmin, along with Jimmy, into the basement by their legs, where he spent the next twelve hours chopping up and dismembering them before he burned and tossed their bodies into the Hudson. Next on his list was Kammron.

T.J. Edwards

Chapter 14

Kammron held baby Coke in his arms and bounced him up and down in a loving fashion. "Yo, now that Bonkers told me all that shit, I gotta admit that he does look just like me. He even got my thick eyebrows." Kammron looked his son over closely. He picked him up under his arms and held him in the air. "You gon' be a boss just like yo daddy, ain't you?"

Henny walked up behind Kammron and placed her hand on his shoulder. "You already know he gon' be just like his damn daddy. How can he not be when y'all got the same DNA?" She tried to kiss Coke on the cheek.

Kammron moved the baby out of the way. "Yo, you be sucking my dick with those lips. Don't be trying to kiss a nigga's prince."

Henny rolled her eyes. "Really, Killa, that's how you feel?"

"I'm just trying to protect my li'l dude, that's all." He held Coke closer to his heart.

"Instead of you making me feel like shit, you should be thanking me for getting him up out of Yasmin's care. She was acting real funny about giving him to me at first, until I told her that you were ready to snap because you wanted to see your son."

"Good fuckin' looking. That nigga Bonkers supposed to be hollering at Jimmy right now, and I don't know if all of that shit gon' spill over to Bonkers and Yasmin's crib. If it does or it doesn't, I don't want my seed nowhere around that shit." He kissed his cheek again and cocked his head back. "Yo, you fart, shorty?"

"N'all, I think that's the baby. I'ma go get his diaper bag so you can change him."

"Change him? Me? Man, you got me fucked up. It's too many bitches in this house for Killa to be changing anybody. Y'all handle my li'l Prince. Get him right. Before you put a pamper on his ass, make sure you give him a bath. After he gets fresh and clean, rub him down with some oils and rock him to sleep, whispering and letting him know that he is a king in the making. Do I make my muthafuckin' self clear?"

Henny nodded. "As you wish, daddy. You know I got you." She carried Coke away.

Reyanna stopped at the doorway and waited until Henny walked past her. Then she stepped into the room. "Daddy, Duke Da God just pulled up outside. He said for you to come out there so he can holler at you."

Kammron grabbed her by her blouse and brought her to him. He kissed her kips savagely, and gripped her ass. He slid his hands under her skirt and pulled her thong to the side with his fingers. They found her hole. He slipped them inside. "Why you walking around dis mafucka with an attitude? You got somethin' you wanna say to me?" He dug his fingers deep and slowly pulled them out, rubbing them on her lips. He kissed her with his fingers in the middle of them.

Reyanna shook her head. "Nall, daddy, I'm good. If had somethin' to say to you, I would say it. You grant me that freedom."

Kammron stuck his fingers into her mouth and made her suck them dry. Then he tongued her down. "Yo, you sleeping wit' me tonight. Daddy gon' spend some quality time wit' you since we ain't touched bases in a minute. You good wit that?" He was rubbing all over her ass again.

She nodded. "Yes, daddy, that's all I need. I've been feeling so lost and alone here lately. I can stand for some catering too. Is that too much to ask?" She looked into his eyes, and wrapped her arms around his waist.

"I ain't say shit 'bout catering to you. You sleep wit me, we fuckin' all night. You already know what dem Percs and dat dog food do to a nigga. So don't get shit twisted. But we most definitely gon' do our thing. I think at the very least you deserve that. For now, take yo ass in there and cater to my son beside Henny. I want my li'l nigga rubbed down, and massaged like a Prince. Then you hoes need to sing him a lullaby, word up. Go handle that, now." She was about to walk off when Kammron grabbed her by the blouse and pulled her back to him. He tongued her down slowly with his hands gripping her fat booty that poked out from her lower back like a full stomach.

When they broke the kiss, Reyanna smiled. "I can't wait until tonight. I've been real patient. All I want is my turn, that's all." She left the room.

***

Duke Da God stepped out of his silver Range Rover, with the mirror tints and walked up Kammron's steps. He met him on the porch and hugged him. "What it do, kid?"

There were Harlem snipers ducked off in trees and in four of the surrounding houses, watching Kammron and Duke real closely. They had already been given the order that if ever anything looked fishy, they should shoot first and ask questions never. Those were Kammron's exact orders.

"Duke, it's ten o'clock at night. Fuck is you doing here? I'm spending time wit' my family."

"Yo', I got two people in the truck that are about to blow yo' mind. I didn't want to bring them here, but they insisted. They already knew ya residence and all of that shit. Look, Dunn, I ain't gon' say no more. Peep this." Duke reached for the handle to the back passenger's door of his whip and opened the door.

Ashley stepped out of it with a short, tight fitting Dolce and Gabbana skirt dress that clung to her body. She nervously walked up to Kammron with her blue eyes eyeing him the whole time. She stopped in front of him. "I had to see you. I needed to. I can't stop thinking about you, ever since that night. I want you, Kammron. Please don't turn me down. My mother, Elaine, is here, too. We both need you."

Duke smiled. "I told you that you wasn't finna believe me, nigga." He held out his hand, and Elaine stepped out of the truck with a tight, red Burberry dress acting as a second skin. Her double D breasts looked as if they were trying to bust out of it.

Kammron grabbed a handful of Ashley's hair. She yelped. He pulled her to him by it. "Bitch, you think you can pop up on me whenever you feel like it? Huh? You think yo li'l pink ass get special privileges a somethin'?"

"No. I-I-I don't. I just thought that..." Ashley stammered.

Kammron yanked up her skirt and slipped his hand under it. He was surprised to find her without panties. He slipped his finger into her bald pussy and wormed it in and out. She was already dripping wet. "You like that, bitch?"

She closed her eyes. "Mmm, yes." Ashley's tongue crept out of her mouth and traced her lips.

"Yo, Duke, we finna flip these hoes on some Harlem shit. After we're done, they ain't finna be able to look at each other in the morning." Kammron sucked on Ashley's neck.

Duke Da God nodded. "I'm down for whatever, word to Uptown."

***

Kammron took off his Ralph Lauren button up and tossed it onto the floor of the Trump hotel. He slid his boxers down and stepped out of them. Elaine pulled her bra off of her breasts and allowed for the material to fall on the floor. Her big titties bounced around on her chest. She came over to Kammron, and knelt beside Ashley on the floor. Ashley pumped Kammron's dick with her small right hand. It grew in her fist. She pulled it closer to her and sucked on the head hungrily. Her pussy was so wet that it dripped down her inner thighs.

"Yo, you bitches want some of the king, y'all finna take turns sucking me off. Gon' head and pop that out of yo' mouth, Ashley, and give it to Elaine."

Ashley swallowed him whole and popped him out. She held his dick out for Elaine. Elaine took it and sucked it right into her mouth, tasting Ashley's spit along with Kammron's naturalness. She moaned as she sucked him. Kammron played with both of their titties. All four nipples were rock hard and extended, ready for more pleasure.

Duke got down and made Elaine bend over on all fours. He got behind her and slid into her pussy while he fingered Ashley. Ashley gasped and watched his fingers go in and out of her. She sucked harder and faster on Kammron in anticipation of what was to come next.

Kammron grabbed her by her hair and dragged her a short distance away from Duke. He laid her down on the carpet and rubbed her pink pussy. The plump lips were seeping her juices. Her clit stood out like a hard nipple at the top of her slit. Kammron thumbed it. He opened her up and watched her tiny hole appear. He fingered it at full speed. Her breasts shook on her chest.

Duke forced Elaine's face to land on Ashley's breasts. "Suck her titties, bitch. We know how you snow bunnies get down." He fucked her harder.

"Unnnnn!" Elaine flicked her tongue out at Ashley's nipples. Afraid of what might happen to her, and lost in the heat of the moment, she sucked Ashley's nipple into her mouth and pulled on it while Duke Da God long stroked her from behind.

Ashley pushed her face away. She sat up and pulled Kammron down. Kammron climbed between her thighs and lined himself up. He slammed into her and proceeded to fuck her so hard that he was forced to close his eyes.

"Aww. Aww. Aww. Shit. Awwww. Aww. Fuck," Ashley moaned, wrapping her ankles around Kammron's waist while he drilled her.

Kammron bit into her neck and rolled his back. Her pussy felt tighter than before. More wet. It made noises that drove him crazy. "Yeah bitch," he growled.

"Unn. Unnn. I wanna see. I wanna see him fuck her," Elaine moaned. She crawled forward on her knees with Duke Da God hitting her from behind. When her face was close enough to see Kammron's dick roughly going in and out of Ashley, she shivered and slammed back on Duke as hard as she could, taking him deep. "Uhhh. He's fuckin' her. He's fuckin' my baby," she screamed. Then she snuck her face between Ashley's thighs and licked the base of Kammron's dick as it plunged in and out of Ashley, saturated with her juices.

Kammron watched her tongue swipe and opened Ashley's pussy lips wider. He trembled. He'd never seen anything so freaky in all of his life. He pulled all the way back, until just his dick head was inside of Ashley, and forced Elaine's face into his crotch. She licked up and down his dick, pulled it out and sucked it into her mouth. Then she guided it back into Ashley, and allowed for Kammron to fuck her some more before she pulled it and deep throated it like a professional. Once again, she guided it back into Ashley. Kammron, got to tearing Ashley up, remembering what Elaine had just done. He growled and fucked her hard.

Duke plunged into Elaine and shivered. "Aw fuck. Fuck, fuck, fuck." He pulled his piece out and came all over her booty and back. He slapped her ass and came some more, fingering her asshole.

Kammron dove deep. Ashley screamed and dug her nails into his back. She screamed and licked his neck. Kammron came in large jets, over and over, splashing her walls. He pulled his dick out and fed it to Elaine. She sucked him with no hands. Her face moved back and forth. She slurped and played with her own pussy.

Ashley laid back with her sex lips wide open. She slipped her middle finger into herself and ran it in and out. Her plump lips would open as she pulled the finger out and fold inward when she pushed it into herself. She humped into the air. "More, Kammron, please."

Kammron, flipped her over and laid her flat out on her stomach. He opened her ass cheeks and spit directly on her rose bud. He put his dick right on the eye of it and began to work it into her slowly.

Ashley clawed at the carpet, trying to get away. "Wait. No. Please. Uhhhhh."

Kammron bucked forward and slammed deep into her. Her ring reluctantly opened around him. He took a hold of her hips, pulled her to all fours, and spaced her knees apart. "Bitch, eat her pussy now, before I smoke you," he snapped at Elaine.

Elaine slipped under her upside down and took a hold of her pussy lips. She opened them and sucked on Ashley's clitoris. Her tongue played circles around it.

"Unnnnnnnnn," Ashley moaned. She came, feeling Kammron stuff her and Elaine sucking on her tender clitoris. She slammed back into Kammron and moaned loudly. Her scent filled the room. "Fuck me. Fuck me, Kammron. Fuck my ass. Fuck it. Awww shiittt, mommy, you're so disgusting!" Elaine's tongue manipulated her clit again and she came hard, falling on top of Elaine, humping into her face.

Kammron pulled her back up and fucked her for thirty minutes straight, until he came again. Then he pushed her off of him and bussed all over her and Elaine, with a mug on his face. He stood up and dumped Moët on both of them, before drinking from the bottle. "You bitches go run my bath water. I need to be washed up."

***

When he got home that night, Reyanna was waiting in the bed for him. She was up, with her cellphone in front of her face, reading a book on Kindle by Jelissa Shante, her favorite writer. She put it down and looked up to Kammron. "I hope you are not mad at me for being in your bed. You did say that you and I were going to spend some time together tonight."

Kammron was exhausted. He yawned and covered his mouth. "You good, shorty. He took his shirt off and tossed it into the hamper. He carried his pistol to the bed and slid in under his pillow. He yawned again. "So what are you looking for here?"

Reyanna felt offended. "I don't know. I just thought maybe you could hold me for a little while. That's all I really want. You're always so busy."

"A mafucka can't make no major money being still. Niggas that got a lot of time on their hands ain't got no money. Mafuckas that ain't got no time keep they hands on major money. I'm feeding over a thousand niggas right now. That's men and women. That's why I'm always busy." He stripped down and climbed in the bed. He was beyond tired.

Reyanna pulled back the covers and allowed him to get inside of them. When he was lying next to her, she pulled them back up and hugged up next to him. "I understand that you got a lot going on, Kammron."

"It's daddy. Don't call me by my name. I feed yo ass, clothe you, make sure that you're taken care of at all times. That's what father's do. You feel me?"

"Yes, daddy."

He slid his arm under her neck and hugged up with her. "Awright, now what were you about to say?"

"I was just going to say that I understand that you are very busy. You are doing a lot and there are so many people that are thankful for you, including myself. I guess I just get lonely at times. You mean a lot to me, daddy. Especially since you are the only family that I have now. I feel myself becoming so vulnerable that I hate it."

Kammron's eyelids were so heavy that he was struggling to keep them open. "Yo, you my baby. I fuck wit you the long way." He closed his eyes and snapped them back open. They grew heavy again. "All you gotta do is play yo muthafuckin' role. You are sleeping next to the king of Harlem. You are in the best position that you could ever be in." He kissed her cheek and slipped his hand into her panties, cuffing her pussy.

Reyanna cocked her thighs wider for him. "Okay, daddy. I can see that you're tired. So I'ma let you sleep. Do you think we can make this day up tomorrow a somethin'?"

Kammron was knocked out. He snored lightly. Reyanna looked him over and shook her head. She snuggled closer to him and hugged up before going to sleep as well.

Chapter 15

Kammron opened and blinked his eyes. Slowly but surely his vision came into focus. Henny stood on the side of the bed with her arms crossed and a mug on her face. She glared at him with angry eyes. "Killa, why the fuck she get to sleep in the bed with you last night? Is it 'cause I'm on my period?"

Kammron sat up and stretched his arms above his head. "Fuck is you talking bout, Henny? Damn, you getting on my mafuckin' nerves too early."

Henny pointed at Reyanna. "That bitch is sleeping in the bed with you. How the fuck am I the queen of the set when this bitch sleeping next to you, snoring, all happy and shit. You got ya big ass hand down her panties. What the fuck, Killa?"

"Henny, word to Jehovah, man, I'm seconds away from getting up and bussing yo ass. Shut the fuck up. I ain't even had my fix yet."

Henny pulled a syringe filled with heroin out of her bra and tossed it at him. "Huh. Now get yo ass up and tell me what the fuck is going on."

Reyanna finally stopped faking like she was sleeping and sat up. "You always gotta cause some type of drama. Damn. You spend time with him all the time. You act like nobody else can chill wit' him. That shit is so weak." She slid out of the bed and slipped her nightgown over her head.

Henny rushed into her face. "Bitch, watch yo' mouth when you speak to a boss bitch, before I scrape you. Ain't no pussies over here, word up."

Reyanna balled her fists. "Say, Henny, I got mad respect for you and all of that. You brought me to Kammron. I got a place to stay and lay my head. He takes care of me. I appreciate all of that. But you ain't finna keep talking to me like it's sweet. Straight up. I'm good wit these hands. I ain't lost too many fights."

Henny sucked her teeth and pushed her so hard that she went flying into the lamp stand. The lamp flew off of the table and crashed to the floor. Reyanna cut her arm and hollered out in pain. "Punk ass bitch, let's get it then." Henny threw her guards up.

Reyanna came to her feet. She looked at her arm. Blood ran down it. She mugged Henny. "Okay then, this what you wanna do?" She rolled her head around on her neck.

Kammron pulled the syringe out of his arm and set it on the dresser. He smiled and ran his hand over his face. He looked over to the girls. They were squared up, ready to go at each other. "Yo, while you hoes over there acting real stupid, who the fuck watching my Prince?"

"I just put him to sleep, after feeding him. He gon' be good for at least two hours. We good. I'm finna whoop this bitch," Henny announced.

Kammron stepped over to them. He looked down at Henny. "Yo, so you running shit now?"

She didn't even bother with looking up at him. "Nah, kid, I don't run nothin', but I ain't about to let this bitch walk around this mafucka thinking she better than me. I'm Queen B, word up, so move so I can whoop her ass."

Kammron laughed. With surprising speed, he grabbed Henny by the neck and lifted her into the air. He carried her across the room and planted her up against the wall. She hit at his hands and kicked at his ribs. Kammron was so high that he couldn't feel any of it. "Now you listen to me. I run you, and I run that caramel bitch over there. You hoes run under me. If I wanna sleep with her, then I can. Bitch, if I want you to sleep with her ass naked, that's what you gon' do. Now do I make myself perfectly clear? Huh?" He squeezed harder.

Henny wiggled her legs. She fought to breathe. She nodded her head as best she could while in his grasp. Her vision began to go blurry.

Kammron dropped her. She fell to the floor, coughing and choking. She crawled on her knees with tears running down her cheeks. She looked up to Kammron. "Why, Killa? Why you doing me like this in front of these hoes? I'm supposed to be your li'l baby. Don't that mean nothing?"

Kammron grabbed a change of clothes. "You are. I don't like you running around this mafucka wit' a chip on yo' shoulder, though. There can only be one person in charge at all times. That's me. I don't share my throne wit no nigga, or bitch. That shit ain't happening. Clean up this mafuckin' room before I get out of the shower." He left the room.

Reyanna came over and stood in front of Henny. She held her hand out for her to grab a hold of. "Henny, please, take it."

Henny glared at her and stood up. She stepped in her face. "What you got to say about that, huh? You think you the top bitch now?"

Reyanna shook her head. "Girl, what the hell are we doing here?"

"Say what?" Henny was thrown off by her question.

Reyanna looked past her shoulder. She hurried and closed the door. Then she came back and stood in her face. "Look, Henny, I swear I don't have anything against you. I don't wanna be some top bitch, or whatever you just said. I just wanna be happy, and I don't see that happening for me or you here. I think the smart move for us is to get out of here while we are still alive."

"And go where? You sound so stupid right now. Kammron run the fuckin' city. This owns Harlem, and now he's slowly taking over Queens. Before it's all said and done, he will be in New York. Where the fuck are we going to go?"

She bumped her out of the way and started to clean up the room.

"I have ten thousand dollars in my trust fund. It's not much, but it will get us out of this state. Once we are out of New York, we can go anywhere. I'm telling you that it is in our best interest to do so. I love you, and I don't wanna see you hurt."

"You wanna know what I don't wanna see?" Henny stood up with the broken piece of the lamp in her hand. "I don't wanna see you sleeping in my man's bed. I don't wanna see you walking around this mafucka like you own it. And I don't wanna near you trying to get me to commit treason to the set. Bitch, play yo role, or lose yo mafuckin' life. Fuck you thought this was?" Henny's chest heaved up and down.

"You know what, Kammron has got you brainwashed. You're out of your freaking mind and it's just a matter of time before he kills you. I can't even say that it'll be his fault. He's just naturally evil, and you're equally dumb." She shook her head. "Fuck off." She started to clean up the room beside Henny with plans of escaping Kammron on her mind.

"Yeah, bitch, whatever. I hope you do leave. I'll have my man all to myself."

"You're too stupid to see that you will never have Kammron. He is more in love with himself than he could ever be with anybody else. I see that, and that's why I gotta get out of here."

"Well hurry up. Fuck taking you so long?" Henny spat.

"I ain't going nowhere without you. Despite how you feel about me, I love yo' stubborn ass."

Kammron burst into the room holding his phone and looking over the Facebook article with a smile on his face. "Jimmy dead. That bitch nigga is gone. Yasmin and Yazzy too. Damn. When the fuck did this happen?" He laughed and sipped from his bottle of Moët.

Henny rushed and took the phone out of his hand. "What? This can't be. I was just talking to her." She continued to read. When she was convinced that they were talking about Jimmy, Yasmin, and Yazzy's remains that a fisherman had found, she covered her mouth. "Wow."

"Well, at least I ain't gotta worry about no custody battle for Coke. Look like my li'l nigga gon' be wit me. Henny, baby girl, you are officially his mother. That's yo son. Whew. Let me go get in the water. Tonight, I'm popping bottles. Dat bitch nigga is dead." He left the room again.

Reyanna stepped beside Henny. You telling me that you don't see how crazy this man is? We need to get out of here. New mommy," she scoffed and went back to cleaning up the room.

Henny stood there, stuck in place. She couldn't believe Kammron's reaction. She couldn't believe that Yasmin was gone, and that now Kammron was forcing Coke upon her. She didn't even know if she was ready to have her own child. She definitely wasn't ready to adopt a kid. Suddenly, the things that Reyanna was saying to her began to make sense. She sighed in defeat of the inevitable. "Reyanna, what's the plan?"

***

"Yo, that means that Bonkers smoked all three of them mafuckas. I wonder how he got so sloppy to the point where they were able to identify the bodies," Duke Da God said while sipping from his double cup of Lean. The drink stung his throat as it slid down into his belly. They were sitting inside of his new Porsche truck. Duke had the custom made top peeled back as they overlooked the waves crashing into the shore of the beach.

Kammron sipped his Lean. "Yo, I think Bonkers was fucked up in the head when he found out that neither of the children were his. He snapped. He wanted to get rid of Yasmin and all of them so bad that he did a half ass job. The Feds gon' fuck around and be all over this. Not only that, but Queens is about to go up. Those Jamaicans that Jimmy got in place gon' either fall under Bonkers, or they are about to go against his ass. Either way, we gon' steal some of that territory and label it the new Harlem. Wherever we set up shop will be considered our territory. It'll be Harlem. Our hustlers and bitches will have diplomatic immunity. If a mafucka touches any one of our troops or people from Harlem that's stationed over there in Queens, then the set gon' go into beast mode wit' no mercy. Word to the borough."

Duke Da God, laughed. "Damn, Kammron, you a fool, my nigga. The way you see shit on this conquering level is bananas, word up. My brain doesn't work like that. I can break down some mathematical shit quick, but the divide and conquer shit is definitely mastered by you." Duke held up his cup. "To dividing and conquering New York."

"To Killa sitting atop the throne of New York."

"And Duke at his right hand."

They laughed and bumped cups.

Chapter 16

As expected, as soon as the Jamaicans that Jimmy had in place to take over Queens found out that he had been murdered, anarchy ensued and the borough turned into a complete war zone, with Bonkers in the middle of it. Before Jimmy was killed, he'd ordered for fifty of his deadliest savages from Kingston, Jamaica to follow and fall under Bonkers. Bonkers took them in, along with their families, and he fed the killas. He provided for them and made sure that they never needed for anything.

Slowly but surely their loyalties came to lie with him. Because the war was getting intense and Jimmy was out of commission, Bonkers needed more firepower but he didn't have a supplier for his weapons. With his back up against the wall and trapped inside of the bloodiest of wars that the borough of Queens had ever seen, he reached out to Kammron for assistance.

Kammron rented Bonkers all of Harlem's old and outdated weapons. He gave them guns that already had four and five murders on them. Assault rifles that jammed once they got too hot, and shotguns that needed to be oiled more than usual. Kammron didn't see the use in giving Bonkers all new weapons when he was already sure that when the time was right, he and his crew of savages were going to flip the script and overpower Bonkers and his crew in order to make them follow him and Harlem.

The longer the war stemmed, the more Kammron began to see Queens as new grounds for Harlem to expand into. He didn't see Bonkers as a threat, and Scarface, the Jamaican that Bonkers was warring with, was not a threat to them either. Neither man had enough money to properly war with Kammron.

Kammron had brand new weapons from the military, fresh out of the military crates. He had grenades, bulletproof vests by the boatload. Bullet proof helmets, armor piercing bullets, dynamite, and loyal, suicidal soldiers that were ready to die for him and his borough at any given time. It would have been nothing for Kammron to crush both Bonkers and Scarface at one time, but instead of acting too fast, he decided to sit back and allow them to kill each other off. When the time was right, he was set to make his move.

In the name of capitalizing off of Bonkers' war, Kammron got great intelligence from his troops that were hired to watch the war between Bonkers and Scarface. He would find out who murdered who and then report it back to Agent Bishop. Agent Bishop would in turn give the Intel to his bosses and the shooters would be arrested and convicted accordingly. With Kammron, it was one hand washes the other.

In the second month of the bloody war, Kammron helped Agent Bishop to indict a total of forty members between Bonkers and Scarface's crews. They were booked on charges of corruption, murder, drug dealing, conspiracy, and many other charges. Agent Bishop was slowly making a name for himself by use of Kammron, and he was loving every minute of it. So much so, that after four months of continued success, he decided to throw his hat into the race for becoming the mayor of the city. He told Kammron that he needed more bodies to drop and more arrests to be made. He needed more serious intelligence. The grimier the better.

Kammron went into overdrive. He gave Bonkers pointers on how to annihilate Scarface on all fronts. He supplied him with dynamite, and a few armor piercing bullets, along with the assault rifles to go with them. Bonkers fell into his trap. For two weeks straight, bodies dropped all over Queens. Kammron had his troops recording the events from afar. They would follow the shooters out of the area, and once they knew where they were laying their heads, they reported back to Kammron. Kammron would give the footage and the Intel to Agent Bishop.

In a span of six months, Agent Bishop made two hundred arrests, and assisted in a hundred and eighty speedy convictions. In the eyes of the city, he was doing things that the mayor of New York could not. Kammron used Khabir to invest heavily in Agent Bishop's campaign. He pumped in a total of fifty million dollars through a series of donors. Khabir also got sixty other super donors to come on board. Agent Bishop blitzed the competition, and five months later was elected mayor of New York. Kammron was in Dubai at the time.

***

Kammron placed his arm around Henny's neck and kissed her cheek as they crunched through the white sand of Dubai's beach. It was eighty degrees outside, with a gentle breeze. Kammron carried a bottle of Moët in one hand, and a fat blunt stuffed with Dubai sour marijuana in his other.

"Yo, Henny, I know shit been real whack for you ever since you been fuckin in my bidness, but I wanna let you know that shit is about to change for the greater good. I feel like you put in that work and embraced my son as being yours, like no other woman has. And because of that, I wanna give you the right to call me your man, and I'ma call you my bitch."

Henny cringed. "Dang, Kammron, why I just can't be ya earth, or ya jewel? I'm tired of being your bitch. Plus, I'm older now. I wanted to be treated like those white girls in fairy tale movies."

Kammron laughed. "Shorty, it's a reason they call that shit fairy tale. It's because it's not real. If it was then there would be no reason for women to have to buy into that fantasy, because it would be right in their homes." He kissed the side of her forehead. "What's the matter with being a bitch, anyway? Especially a boss bitch?"

Henny shrugged her shoulders. "I don't know." The sunlight reflected off of the three carat pink, diamonds in her ear lobes, causing them to shimmer. Her Vera Wang dress fluttered in the wind. Kammron had gotten it specially made for her. That and the fifteen thousand dollar toe rings that were on each of the middle toes on her feet. "I guess I just wanna be something more than a bitch or a hoe. I grew out of those derogatory titles."

"Aw, so you think you more than that now, huh?"

Henny nodded. "Yeah, I do. Why, you don't?"

"Let me explain something to you, Henny. When I was born into this world they called my mother, Kathy, a statistic. They told her that I wasn't never gon' be nothin' but a bum ass li'l nigga from Harlem. They called me a loser. A broke ass nigga. A walking corpse, all of that shit. And it didn't matter how many times I told people what my name was, they chose to call me what I reflected. But now, a mafucka can't call me nothing less than a boss. But I made them switch the narrative."

"What are you sayin' without actually saying, daddy?" The air blew and made her curls flutter in the wind.

"What I'm saying is that you ain't got shit. You ain't accomplished shit. You ain't mastered shit. All you are is a broke, black bitch, that's chasing a nigga's bag for as long as he got it. You are a nobody. Why the fuck should I weaken your hustle or your standing in life by calling you something that the rest of the world never will until you make it happen for yourself?" He pulled off of the blunt and handed it to her. "What do you want out of life?"

Henny was shocked at his bluntness. They continued to walk down the beach together. It was packed. The water was a bright blue. Two bikini clad East Indian women jogged around them and kept going. Kammron watched their asses jiggle as they ran.

"I guess I've always wanted to be an actress, or a dancer. I don't really know past those things and, to be honest, I don't even wanna be those. I just wanna sit back and check a bag." She felt guilty for admitting that. "Why, what do you wanna be?"

Kammron laughed. "I'm it. I've always wanted to be a drug lord. I've always wanted to conquer first Harlem, and then New York, before I set out to conquer the world. That's what I'm doing. Harlem is mine. Next is Queens. That will be transformed into Harlem, and then I'm coming for the remaining boroughs before I shoot up the coast. I'm thinking New Jersey is after New York. That's common sense."

"I'm not talkin about illegal stuff, daddy. I'm talking about being a doctor or a lawyer, or something like that. Have you ever had dreams outside of the hood?"

"Fuck nall. Ugh. I'm a hood nigga. I'm okay with that. All that school shit wasn't for me. I didn't like people knowing more than I did, or learning shit at the same time that I did. I wanted to be in control. I wanted to be the principal before I could master the art of being the student. That's just how I am designed. That following shit ain't in me. I gotta be the boss at all times, with nobody to answer to but me." They kept walking. "But you know what, though, li'l baby. Maybe you just like me. Maybe that other shit ain't for you. You a fast money getter like daddy, so I'ma tell you what, I'ma put you in charge of a few strip clubs in Harlem to let you get used to running shit. Then, when it comes to you, whatever you wanna do, I'ma invest in you with these Harlem dollars. Bet."

She smiled. "Bet, daddy." She ran in front of him and wrapped her arms around his neck.

He picked her up and was surprised when he heard her crying. "Baby, what's the matter?"

"I don't wanna be no bitch no more daddy. I don't wanna be a loser or a hoe. I gotta step my game up and rule somethin', like you. That bum shit ain't in me either. I belong to you, daddy." She wrapped her thighs around his waist while he carried her through the beach, kissing on her cheeks.

"Yo, Henny, hand to God, I love you, li'l baby. I love you and I'm fuckin' wit you forever. Daddy promise." He kissed her lips.

Henny hugged him tighter and cried harder. "I love you so much, daddy. I love you with all of my heart."

***

The Yacht floated on top of the sea while Henny laid back on the soft bed that Kammron had pulled out to the bow of the boat. It was covered with one thousand thread count Gucci sheets. Above them was Dubai's dark black sky, and it was full of bright stars that twinkled. Kammron fell between Henny's thick thighs and kissed her lips. They tasted sweet to him. He licked all over them. Two iced Patek watches flooded his left wrist and he had a red iced Rolex on his right. Henny had a pink Patek on her left wrist and two yellow iced Rolexes on her right one. Kammron kissed her again. "Shorty, we are a long way from Harlem."

Henny opened her thighs wide and pulled him into her. "I know, daddy. Can you say it again?' She sat up and licked his lips.

"Say what, baby?" He slipped his hand between her thighs and moved her Fendi underwear to the side so he could feel her silky lips. He bit into her neck.

"Can you tell me that you love me again? Please, I need to hear it."

Kammron snickered. "Yo, like I said before, I love you and I'm fuckin' wit you indefinitely.

She shivered and pulled him down by his shoulders. "Make love to me, daddy. I know you know how to fuck. You got that dick game proper but make love to yo baby girl. That's what I want. Please, daddy." She sucked his earlobe and stuck her tongue inside of it.

Kammron slowly slid into her, leaving her panties in the crux of her thighs. "Mmm, awright, ma. This new territory, but for the first lady of the set, you got this coming. He fucked into her slowly. "I love you, boo. Daddy loves the shit out of you." He pumped some more.

She touched his lips. "Shhhh, no swearing, daddy. Just love." She wrapped her ankles around the small of his back.

Kammron long stroked her, slowly and deeply. "Huh. Huh. Huh. Daddy loves you."

Henny's eyes rolled into the back of her head. She held her mouth wide open and moaned louder and louder. While Kammron had always been able to fuck her into oblivion, the fact that he was actually taking his time to make love to her was driving her crazy and pushing her closer to her climax than ever before. "Say it, daddy. Tell me again."

"I love you, boo. Daddy loves you. You're mine. Mine. Mine. I got you. Me, just me. Huh. Huh. Uhhhh, li'l baby."

Henny arched her back and dug her nails into his back. She screamed loudly. Her screams resonated all throughout the water, before she came hard. She shook.

Kammron plunged deeper and deeper. He grabbed her around the neck and squeezed. He came deep within her, groaning loudly. Then he pulled her on her side, got behind her, and slowly made love to her for the next two hours, telling her over and over again that he loved her. By the end of the session, he had convinced himself that he was telling the truth and had fallen for Henny in a way that he hadn't before. Though the feeling for her met resistance inside of himself, there was also a piece of him that welcomed the intrusion of love into his black heart.

Chapter 17

Bonkers leaned his head down and snorted two thick lines of the North Korean heroin. He sat back on the couch and allowed the drug to take over his system. His mind drifted off. He thought about little Yazzy and the last time he'd been given the chance to spend some time with her. They'd gone to Coney Island and all she kept telling him was that she loved him and how he was the greatest daddy in all of the world. Now she was gone. Murdered by his hands.

He frowned and grabbed the bottle of Hennessey off of the table and downed a quarter of it. He wiped his mouth as both the drug and the liquor coursed through him. "I should've never killed you, Yazzy. You were innocent. Yo mama was the hoe. All you knew was me. I punished you for that." A lone tear fell from his eye. He wiped it away and tooted two more lines of heroin.

Murda came into the room with a Tech .9 in his hand. He stopped in front of Bonkers and looked down on him. "Bruh, you good?" Murda was born and raised in Harlem. He was only eighteen years old, but already proven to be a loyal savage to Bonkers. While most of the borough was running over and falling under Kammron, he took the Bonkers route because he felt like he could get to large sums of money quicker with Bonkers, since there were less people in his entourage.

Bonkers pulled his nose. "I'm good, kid. I was just thinking about my daughter, that's all. I'm missing her like a mafucka."

"I can feel that." Murda was five feet eleven inches tall, dark skinned with a big nose and gray eyes.

"How many losses we took yesterday? Did you get the exact count?" Bonkers drank from his bottle of Hennessy again.

"We lost six more. Twelve have been all over the borough. We need to hit it out of town for a month or so until shit die down, or say fuck it and finally go and holler at Flocka."

Bonkers looked up to him. "You really just said that?"

"I sho' did. That nigga been trying to fuck in yo bidness ever since Jimmy got whacked. He knows you got that hustle shit in yo' bloodline. Yo, word to Harlem, if we go and fuck wit him, we'll sew Queens up like never before. All them off brand ass Jamaicans a have to quit fuckin' wit the other side and fuck strictly wit you, or be wiped out. I mean it's either him or yo day one, Kammron. But that nigga so cocky that he might not be able to offer you shit but a worker slot. I already know you ain't about to go for that."

"That shit ain't even an option." He lowered his head and thought about Kammron. It was ringing all over the city of New York how Kammron had gotten bigger than Nickey Barnes, and all of the Harlem greats. They were saying that he was officially the first dope boy billionaire to ever do it. Bonkers didn't know how true that was, and he definitely didn't think that Kammron had anywhere near a billion dollars, but he was for certain that he was making major moves. Even his workers were all on Facebook, flexing their five hundred thousand dollar cars and jewelry. The women under Kammron rocked expensive clothing, and shoes. They owned businesses and invested their money into the community of Harlem. It was beyond impressive.

Bonkers wondered how things would play out if he ever went to Kammron humbly and asked him to become his right hand man again. He understood that Kammron and Duke Da God were jammed tight and thick as thieves. He didn't think he could penetrate their bond. He was sure it would only breed envy and hate. He couldn't risk it. Besides he felt that if Kammron was able to become a Don by moving one brick at a time, then he would be able to do the same thing.

Murda rubbed his chin. "Say, kid, when yo ass get quiet, I already know that it's a mafuckin' problem. What you got roaming through your noodle right now?"

"Last time you spoke with that nigga Flocka, did he sound like he was on some snake shit to you?"

"Honestly?"

Bonkers nodded. "Yeah."

"Dawg, it sounds to me like he's really trying to have you move into the slot that Jimmy was in. You know my roots go back to the island. That nigga Flocka is live. He's a major made nigga. If you can get kid on board, I'm telling you the sky's the limit for Queens. We'd be able to take over dis bitch, and then come for Harlem. You already know that Harlem is rightfully ours as well."

Bonkers scooted to the edge of the couch, nodding his head. "One thing that Jimmy always told me about the game is that it's not what you know or how much you hustle, but it's who you know. I know damn well that Kammron ain't get to where he is by not using somebody."

"They say he got a Saudi Prince on his team, and a politician. I don't know how true it is, but he force damn near every mafucka in Harlem to vote for Henry Bishop. Now that mafucka is the mayor. That nigga been making major moves and we just been sitting here trapping like the average broke ass dope boy. Fuck that, son, it's time that we level up. What you wanna do?" Murda was hyped up. "I'm bout whatever."

Bonkers sighed loudly. "Set up a meeting with Flocka. Tell that nigga that we need to meet in a mutual spot, where I can know that ain't no foul play involved. Once I can see that he wanna really talk bidness, then it's a go. Word up."

"Yo, say less." Murda pulled out his phone. He dialed Flocka and walked out of the room.

Bonkers stood up. "Ain't shit mediocre about me. I'm a Don. I was made to be a boss, just as much as Kammron. Fuck that nigga, word to Christ. Kid ain't wanna take me wit' him so he finna have to see me. There can only be one king, and that shit is me."

Murda stepped back into the room. "Nigga, pack yo bags. We headed first class to Jamaica, all expenses paid. Flocka ready to get shit moving forward. He promises those M's. That's millions, nigga, just in case you was sleep like a burped baby."

Bonkers mugged him. "I stay woke. Let's handle this shit."

***

Kammron rotated the right handle and increased his speed on the 4 wheeler as he rolled through Harlem with a hundred of his troops behind him. It was Juneteenth, and the city, courtesy of Kammron, was celebrating the ending of slavery. Kammron, headed the pack with three million dollars' worth of jewelry around his neck. Beside him was Duke Da God. Duke's neck was just as chunky. Kammron rocked four Patek watches, flooded in diamonds, two on each wrist. It was a bright and sunny day and the streets were flooded with the residents of Harlem. The majority of the intersections were blocked off, and approved by the city to do so.

Kammron rolled the pack of 4 wheelers all the way to Malcolm X Park and hopped off of it. His troops, made up of women and men, jumped off of their bikes and flooded the park that was full of project women barbecuing and setting up multiple tables with all kinds of side dishes.

Kammron walked through the pack like a true king. His killas were posted in trees, bushes, and all around the park. They were heavily armed and thirsty to kill something for Kammron. They knew that such an act could mean that they had the chance of being catapulted up the ladder of underworld success. And for a killer or a trap star, that was major.

Kammron stopped in the middle of the park and stepped on top of a picnic table. He was fitted from head to toe in Chanel. His double C's had baby diamonds acting as rhinestones. "Yo, everybody shut the fuck up for a second. Be quiet, the king got somethin' to say."

The crowd quieted and slowly moved around the picnic table. The closer they got, the more Kammron's security moved in. They made sure that the crowd was twenty feet back. The security held their assault rifles in their hands eyeing the crowd closely.

Kammron smiled. "Yo, I'm saying right now that it bet not be nothing but Harlem residents up in this mafucka. Ain't nobody about to eat this food, drink our pops, or enjoy our party unless they are from Harlem, so I'm giving out a splash warning right now. If you ain't from Harlem, leave this park, right now."

Kammron looked over the crowd. Slowly but surely a few people began to make their way through the pack of people and out of the park. He waited a bit longer as more people left.

"Anybody else don't deserve to be here?" Nobody moved. He scanned the crowd. "Awright, then. That's mo' like it. We don't do it for nobody but us. Harlem is the center of the universe. We are all family and it's on my shoulders to make sure that my family eat. How y'all feeling out there tonight, though?"

The crowd cheered and grew louder and louder. The security stepped forward to push them back just a bit. Little kids were running back and forward, already bored with Kammron's big speech.

"Yo, we go the earths out there grilling Porter houses and all that good shit. The weed, pills, drinks, and everything in between is heavy for my people. Everybody rent paid, bills crushed, courtesy of the set. Killa just blew four million on his people. Who the king?"

The crowd hollered his name loudly and cheered. Kammron ate it up. It fed his ego. He hopped down off of the table and slipped his arm around Henny's neck. "Say, Goddess, you look real good rocking that Fendi like you doing."

She had on a pink and black Fendi skirt dress that clung to her like a second skin. The diamonds on her fingers and neck were pink VVS's. She had a pink and white diamond crown on her head that read: First Lady. Her nails and toes were French tipped, and behind her were a group of exotic women from Harlem that ran under her Coke Queens crew. They were a crew of female bosses that owned businesses and trapped in the slums just as hard as the men. They did what they did with the backing and security of Kammron and Duke Da God.

Henny pulled her Prada shades low on her nose. "You already know I gotta put on for you, daddy. When they see me, they wonder what this shit like under these clothes, and between these thighs, and the only man that can say that he knows what this shit is like for definite is you."

Kammron kissed her neck. "Bonkers, too, don't forget about that."

Henny scoffed. "That nigga couldn't reach my doorbell to get let into my house. That li'l shit he did was comical. Don't insult me like that, daddy. You already know this pussy is yours."

Kammron gripped her ass. "Yeah, I know that. I love you, shorty. I still mean that shit."

"I love you, too." She stepped on her tippy toes and kissed him on the lips.

Kammron looked past her and saw an array of fine dimes from Harlem jocking him. They looked him over hungrily. He snickered and broke eye contact with them. "Yo, let's enjoy the party. Make sure you keep your eye out for anybody that's trying to crash this bitch. Send yo hoes to do their rounds." He kissed her forehead and walked off.

Duke Da God danced up to him with two bottles of Champagne in his hand. "Kid, this bitch lit. Everybody and they mama at this mafucka." Duke drank from both bottles at one time. "Yo, hand to God, I just checked my bank account after Kamina got done doing his thing, and guess what my shit say, nigga, guess."

Kammron laughed. "I don't know, Duke, what does it say?"

"Five muthafuckin' million. How the fuck do a broke ass kid raised in the slums of Harlem check a bag for five million without rapping or going to the NBA? How nigga?"

"By fuckin' wit the king of Harlem, that's how." Kammron jacked.

"You muthafuckin' right." Duke stepped into Kammron's face. "Word to my soul, I'd die for you, Kammron. I don't give a fuck what we been through in life, I'ma always be down to eat them slugs for you, Dunn. Yo, you a real nigga. That fool, Bonkers, dumb as hell for slipping on this right hand slot. Finders keepers, though." He laughed and held up his bottles.

"Long live King Kammron. The Coke muthafuckin' king." He danced off with his bodyguards following him with their guns out.

Stacie slipped beside him and smiled. She was smoking on a blunt stuffed with OG Kush. Because of the air, the smoke stung her eye. She closed it and pulled off of the blunt. "Kammron, I don't know how you managed all of this, but I am proud of you. I wish my babies were here to see this. I miss them." She spoke in terms of her daughters, Shana and Shelly.

"Yeah, me too. Yo, you need anything Stacie?"

Stacie shook her head. "Boy, you've been giving me five thousand dollars a week for the last two years. What the hell would I need that I ain't already bought myself?" She held out her arms and hugged him. "I love you, though, baby. I might be old, but I'm still a Harlem chick. I can back this thang up, too." She leaned into his ear. "But you know that already don't you, son?" She snickered.

Kammron nodded. "Until my last breath, shorty, you got whatever you need. I love you, too." He pulled her into him and held her for a moment before he let her go.

Henny snuck up beside her with a mug on her face. "Yo', ma, I'm saying, who are you, all up on the god?"

"Excuse me?" Stacie asked, ready to punch, Henny.

"You heard me. I don't know who you is, but I'm the Queen of the set, a Coke Queen, to be exact. I ain't wit' you pressing up on my Don, word up."

Stacie removed her earrings and flicked her blunt into the grass. "Yo, I ain't had a good fight in years, but I'm 'bout to tear this li'l girl up."

Henny's crew stepped behind her. They pulled out their razor blades, ready to slice and dice Stacie. Henny stepped back, about to give the order for them to fuck Stacie over. As soon as Stacie removed her last earring, Kammron stepped up and separated them. Henny mugged him.

"Yo, y'all calm ya asses. This my mother. She got a right to be hugging the kid." He laughed. "Ma, this my shorty. Her name is Henny, and the reason she is so crazy is because she is under my domain, and has been ever since she was a li'l girl."

"I don't care who she is or how many of these li'l nappy headed girls she thinks rolling with her. She better respect me, or we gon' have it out. I'm an original Harlem Queen. Kammron you better tell her."

"No doubt about it. Yo blood bleed the borough, word to my Queens right here. It's all love, just one big misunderstanding." He kissed Stacie on the cheek, and nudged her toward the crowd. "I'll rub elbows wit' you later, Goddess."

"Okay." Stacie mugged Henny as she made her way past her. Then her eyes were on all of Henny's crew.

Henny sucked her teeth. "Man..." She stepped toward Stacie.

Stacie kept walking. "You betta gon' li'l girl, and listen to yo man." She waved her off. "I'll take this shit back to the eighties." She kept mumbling as she disappeared through the crowd.

Kammron snatched Henny to him. "I love this new animal. Word up. You got mad heart for the god. That's all love."

"Daddy, you gon' make me kill one of these hoes over you. I don't wanna do it, but if I have to, I will." She scanned the crowd. "I'm finna go and enjoy myself because the longer I stay in your presence, the more trouble I'm gon' wind up getting into. Let's roll ladies." She waved bye to him and mobbed through the crowd.

"Damn, I created a monster." Kammron laughed and went to get him a plate.

That evening, the folks of Harlem ate, smoked, and drank good. They danced. They laughed. They burped from full bellies, and had a good time. Kammron spared no dollar to make sure that his people were well taken care of. This was his borough, and they meant everything to him.

Chapter 18

Kingston, Jamaica

Bonkers sat in the Cabaña on the beach as the blue ocean water crashed into the sand loudly. Beside him was Murda. Murda wore dark shades. Bonkers looked over at him and nodded. Murda nodded back and continued to scan the beach, looking for any potential threats that may have tried to blindside Bonkers or him in any way.

Bonkers yawned. "What time Kid said he'd be here again?"

Murda checked the time on his phone. It read six 'clock. "He should be coming up any minute now."

As if on cue, Flocka appeared at the edge of the beach. He had two gorgeous Jamaican women with him, one was dark skinned and the other light skinned and stacked. He strolled through in the sand with an air of confidence. His long dreadlocks fell to his waist. The tips were golden, as if he'd dyed them. Across his face was a pair of Dior glasses with black tints. He walked into the Cabaña with his hand out. He extended it. "Bonkers, mon, it's a pleasure."

Bonkers shook his hand, standing up. "The pleasure is all mine. It took you long enough to get here, though, didn't it?'

"When you are as deep in the game as I am, moving about the way a man wants to becomes a little more difficult. Not everybody is a fan of Flocka. May I?" He asked, waving his hand over a seat.

"Please." Bonkers sat across from him and held up a bottle of Moët. "You sipping?"

"Sure." Flocka took a hold of the bottle and poured some into the glass that Murda provided him. "Thank you." He gave the bottle back to Bonkers.

"Now that I'm here, what's on your mind, Flocka?"

"First, I must give you my sincerest condolences for the loss of Jimmy. I know that you two were close and I can only imagine what you are going through." Flocka held up his glass as the two beauties that had come along with him stood outside of the Cabaña on security. Each woman had an assault rifle in her hands and wouldn't hesitate to use it with a murderous intent.

"Thank you for expressing that, but I come from thick skin. Death is a part of the game, and we must move on. Why am I here?" Bonkers drank from the bottle.

"Before Jimmy was killed, and we're still investigating that whole dilemma, but before he was taken away, Jimmy was set to take over Queens on Jamaica's behalf. I have invested a total of two million plus dollars into that borough. Money that Jimmy was supposed to use to get a strong standing within New York. Before he was killed, I feel like he was making progress." Flocka smiled. His mouth was full of gold.

"Once again, why am I here? Do you think that I am going to pay Jimmy's debts, or somethin'?" Bonkers said this as a sly joke, but Flocka didn't laugh.

"Two million dollars may not be much money in New York, but in Jamaica, it is enough to feed an entire village for a year. With the ground that Jimmy was making, I was looking forward to relocating my people to Queens, as well as using the flip of the money to strengthen my people's lives here on the island. I am a very proud man. I love my country, and I love my people. What I don't like is to be fucked over by you, or nobody else."

Bonkers adjusted himself in his seat. "It sounds to me like you making statements that you aren't too sure about. I'ma need you to clean that shit up and quick."

Flocka laughed. Now the sun was shining directly off of his gold teeth. "Bonkers, in Jamaica it is forbidden for a drug lord to trust any man outside of the island. With that being said, I want you to know that, not only did I have Jimmy's home bugged and recorded at all times, but so was Yasmin's. I know what took place on those nights. I watched the footage over a thousand times." He drank from his glass. "You sure this is a conversation that you would like to have around your friend here?"

Bonkers felt his heart beating faster in his chest. "We came down here together. We gon' leave together. Say whatever you wanna say. I'm all ears."

"Is that right? Okay, well here goes it." Flocka downed the rest of the glass. "What was it that spawned you to kill Jimmy? Was it the fact that he was fuckin' Yasmin behind your back, or were you envious of his lifestyle?"

"Never envious. That bitch nigga crossed me and he had to pay. I don't give a fuck who anybody is. It's respect first, and that's as simple as that. Jimmy was a snake, so I put his ass under the dirt where he belonged. What, nigga, you called me down here so you can seek retribution?"

Flocka shook his head. "N'all, that's some family shit that y'all had going on. That doesn't concern me. What does concern me is the fact that my money got caught up in the cross fires. My investments, and the imminent future of my people. You gon' have to clean that up, Bonkers."

"Oh yeah? And how might you propose I do that?" Bonkers wished he was armed. He would have gunned Flocka down along with his two body guards that were built like strippers.

"You, Bonkers, are going to come work for me. Since you killed Jimmy, you're going to take his spot and continue the mission that I had for him. And don't get me wrong, it ain't all work. Jimmy had the time of his life. He built up his bank account very fast, and was able to go places that he had never been before. He got a pretty sweet deal. That same deal I am willing to offer you, with two stipulations."

"First of all, before we even get to those stipulations, why me? Why can't you use any other nigga to step in and take over your operations out there in Queens? Especially if you're supplying everything?" Bonkers was getting angry.

"We might as well get to the stipulations first. Which are: number one, I wanna see my people heavily populating Queens, more than ever. You'll learn why later. And secondly, I want this headache, Kammron, crushed, and Harlem under my belt. And I refuse to deny myself either one of these things."

Bonkers leaned toward him. "What you got against, Kammron?"

Flocka made a disgusted face. "Kammron is the number one threat to our advancement. He is cocky, arrogant. He doesn't want to sit down and have boss conversations. He's a separatist. Instead of him uniting the people on all fronts, he chooses to segregate his people of Harlem. He thinks that they are all God's gift to humankind, and he's blown up too fast. He skipped steps. Me, personally, I don't like him, that thug that he's running with, or the borough of Harlem. One of my first priorities when all of this comes into fruition will be to make all of those residents pay for Kammron's transgressions. These are my terms."

"You do know that I am from Harlem, right?" Bonkers eyed Flocka closely.

"If you were from Harlem, they wouldn't do you like they've been doing you for the last year." Flocka laughed. "You get a load of this guy?" He snickered at his security women. They laughed at him, and went back to having serious faces, on high alert.

"Fuck is you talking about? What have they been doing to me for the last year?" Bonkers was ready to snap out.

Flocka shook his head. "You can't be this dumb." He looked Bonkers over. "Oh wow, you really don't know, do you?"

Bonkers shook his head. "What am I missing?"

Flocka scooted forward until he was as close to Bonkers as he possibly could be. "Kammron, Duke Da God, and Harlem have been targeting you ever since you took the throne of Queens. They've been sending jack boys and hit squads to demolish your operations. Kammron is directly connected to the former Agent Bishop, of the Federal Bureau of Investigations. He has had a hand in more than a few of your people being indicted and hung out to dry by the authorities. You see, Kammron is not only playing in the streets. He is also playing the snitching game. Whenever he feels that another crew is in his way, he knocks them out of the box by any means necessary. You are nothin' more than filth to him. He's been picking off your second rate Cartel as if it was child's play. While you had your head up your ass, trying to seek revenge on Jimmy, Kammron was the one fucking Yasmin while you were in a coma, and taking over Harlem, only to leave you behind like a peasant. There is so much that you're too stupid to catch that I now wonder if you really are fit to be the man that I use to take over Queens. This may be me making a major mistake. You see, I would do it on my own, but your government has made it perfectly clear that if I am caught so much as two feet inside of America, any official that sees me has a shoot to kill order in place. It's a long story." He smiled. His dark skinned face lighting up.

Bonkers scrunched his face. He started to replay over all of the events that had taken place within the last year. One by one, each move against him and his crew began to play out in his mind. The attacks against him were sinister in nature, calculated. And it seemed that his adversaries were always a step ahead of him at all times. He felt angry. "How sure are you about all of this shit?"

Flocka smiled. "Kammron is new money, and he's been in the game only for a little while. I am a seasoned vet. You think he's the only one that can buy public officials or get access to sacred footage that is kept from the rest of the world?" He laughed out loud. "Yeah, the fuck, right. Money makes the world go round. Power is in the number behind your digital accounts. You are only as powerful as your political connections. Your reach must extend beyond the shores of America, or you are nothing. I've been doing this shit twenty-five years strong, without a loss. I refuse to take one now." He scooted so close to Bonkers that his knee was touching his. "Rude Boy, you grew up with Kammron. You know him better than anybody else. His habits, his ways, his thoughts, his weaknesses. You are going to at first conquer Queens, then Harlem, and then I will sit back and watch you crush Kammron. After he is crushed, you will be catapulted to the top of the game with us Rastafarians backing you one hundred percent. If ever you wanted to be your own man, now is the time."

Bonkers mugged him. "And if I decline."

Flocka stood up and tapped him on the shoulder. "You won't. The opportunity is worth the rewards. Now come. You will stay in Jamaica for the next month. Get acquainted with our people. You will be treated like royalty. After this month your allegiances will be to Jamaica. Kammron will be crushed. Let's go."

Bonkers sat still for only a moment, thinking about everything that Flocka had told him. Then he got up and followed behind Flocka and his security, with murder and revenge on his mind. Murda walked beside him with his eyes straight forward. Both men were excited and ready for the next level of events.

T.J. Edwards

Chapter 19

Henny pulled the covers off of her and sat on the edge of the bed. She pat her head, before digging her finger inside of her braids to get to the itching spot that was driving her crazy. She looked back at Kammron. He laid flat out with his eyes closed. The covers were pulled down to his waist. His heavily tattooed torso was on full display. She yawned and stretched her arms over her head.

Reyanna knocked on the door lightly, and then pushed it open. She stuck her head inside, thankful to see that Henny was already awake. "Spsst." She waved for her to come.

Henny frowned and ignored her for a moment. She looked back at Kammron and pulled the sheet over his frame. Even though she knew that Kammron was screwing Reyanna, she still didn't like for Reyanna to be able to ogle him whenever Kammron was in her presence. She was the Queen, Reyanna, was nothing more than a nobody. That's how she felt.

"Henny. Girl, come here." Reyanna waved for her to come again.

Henny got up off of the bed, feeling groggy. She strolled across the room and grabbed her night coat off of the back of the closet door. She put it on and met Reyanna in the hallway, after she closed Kammron's master bedroom door behind her.

"Girl, why the fuck are you waking me up this early in the morning. What is the matter with you?"

Reyanna went into her pocket and pulled out two ultrasound pictures. She smiled, happily. "Look."

Henny grabbed the pictures from her and looked them over. "Whose are these?"

"Mine, I'm twelve weeks." She placed her hand on top of her belly.

"That's what's up." Henny kept looking at the pictures. She was about to give them back and then her stomach dropped. "Wait a minute. Who is the father?"

Reyanna took the pictures back. "That's the stupidest question you ever asked me. You already know who it is." She looked over Henny's shoulder. "I'm about to go and tell him right now. Man, I'm so happy." She started to walk around Henny.

Henny blocked her path and guided her down the hallway, away from Kammron's master bedroom. "Girl, are you sure? You mean to tell me that you ain't been messing with no other man other than Killa?" Henny felt like she was ready to throw up. How was Reyanna pregnant before her? Over the last few months, she'd been doing everything in her power to get pregnant with Kammron's seed. She felt that would forever cement her within his heart.

"Girl, you already know that Kammron doesn't play. He ain't about to let us mess around with nobody outside of him. He's the only man that I have ever been with. Now excuse me, I gotta let him know what it is."

Henny pushed her back. She stuck her finger in her face. "Bitch, listen to me. You are not about to tell him you are pregnant. If you tell him, he is going to snap out. We got too much going on right now. That shit ain't happening. Kammron needs to be focused on what he got going on. Besides, I'm the Queen. That means that I am in charge of all of you hoes. That includes you. Take yo ass in your room until we can come up with a solution for this baby." She guided her toward the room that she was staying in.

Reyanna spun out of her guidance. She stopped defiantly in the middle of the hallway. "Henny, I don't know what's wrong with you but you need to get the hell out of my way before I am forced to get on that bullshit with you. Now, I have been very patient and respectful ever since I've been living with y'all, but enough is enough. You are testing my patience."

Henny grew furious. "Aw, so you think you're all big and bad now that you're havin' Kammron's baby? Really, bitch?"

"And you mad 'cause you ain't? What's wrong with you, anyway, huh? That nigga be fuckin' you every day, bussing inside of you, and you still ain't never came up pregnant with his kid. You sure you ain't dead on the inside, or maybe it's all of the dope that you do that's made yo' ass sterile." Reyanna stepped into her face. "I've watched many movies with this whole royalty type shit and I know that a queen can't be a queen unless she is able to have a man's seed. Don't look like you gon' be able to do that no time soon, or at least not before me. Therefore, I got a chance to bump you out of yo' slot. But don't worry, I ain't gon' treat you half as bad as you treated me while I was the low woman on the totem pole." Reyanna got so close that her forehead rested up against Henny's. "Get yo worthless ass out of my way so I can go and tell my baby daddy the good news."

Henny held her head down as all of her anger, jealousy, and frustration came flowing through her all at once. She cocked back and pushed Reyanna with all of her strength. Reyanna went flying backward. She wound up on her back by the entrance to the kitchen. Henny ran and jumped over her. She grabbed a steak knife out of the wooden knife holder and ran back into the hallway where Reyanna was just getting up.

Reyanna held her rib. "You're evil, Henny. You're an evil, sadistic, bitch."

"Pack yo shit right now and get the fuck out of my man's house. If I ever catch you sniffing around him again, or if you ever tell him about that punk ass baby that's growing inside of you, I will kill you. I will haunt you down and make a spectacle out of taking your life. You have my word on that."

Reyanna eyed her with hatred. "You know what, Henny? You can have him because the way I see it, none of this is going to last anyway, and you most definitely need him more than I ever will. I will make my own way in life. I don't need some man, so fuck you and fuck Kammron. Both of y'all can kiss my ass."

Kammron stuck his head out of the bedroom door. "What she just say?"

Reyanna froze with her eyes bucked. "Nothing, I was just goofing off."

Kammron mugged her and then looked over at Henny. "Put that bitch in her place, then come and jump in the shower with me. I need to feel your brown skin for a minute." He slipped into the bathroom.

Henny glared at Reyanna. "Bitch, you got ten minutes to get the fuck out of here, and be thankful that I ain't killing you right now."

Reyanna nodded. "Okay, Henny, you got that. Let me just get my things and I'll be on my way." Reyanna headed into her bedroom and closed the door.

As soon as the door closed, tears dropped from Henny's eyes. Her throat got tight. She wondered if there was something really wrong with her. She walked into the living room and sat on the arm of the couch with her head hung. "What the fuck is life?"

Reyanna came out of the bedroom with a .45 in her hand. She stormed into the hallway with her eyes blazing with anger. She headed to the bathroom and opened the door. Kammron was inside lathering himself up with his body wash. He heard the door open and smiled. "Bout time yo ass hurried up. I got some shit I gotta handle, and I need a quick shot of my baby first."

Reyanna closed her eyes and took a deep breath. "I'm tired of being your bitch, Kammron. I'm tired of you treating me like shit!" She waited for Kammron to pull back the shower curtain with a look of shock and disbelief on his face. She aimed at him and started shooting with the intent to kill.

***

There was a full moon in the sky when Bonkers pulled up in front of Kammron's mansion at eleven o'clock in the evening with fifteen cars and trucks rolling beside and behind him. Bonkers stepped out of his Range Rover dressed in black fatigues, and a black ski mask. In his hand was a hundred round Draco. The Jamaicans that accompanied him wore the same attire as Bonkers, all were strapped and ready for war.

Bonkers stepped in front of Kammron's mansion with a grenade in his left hand. All of the things that Flocka had put him up on was going through his mind all at once. How could Kammron have betrayed him in such a way? How could he himself have been so stupid? The more he thought about it, the angrier he got. He took the grenade and pulled the pin out of it, tossing it as hard as he could through Kammron's front window. "It's war, bitch nigga, and there can only be one king!"

To Be Continued...
Coke Kings 5
Coming Soon

T.J. Edwards

Submission Guideline

Submit the first three chapters of your completed manuscript to ldpsubmissions@gmail.com, subject line: Your book's title. The manuscript must be in a .doc file and sent as an attachment. Document should be in Times New Roman, double spaced and in size 12 font. Also, provide your synopsis and full contact information. If sending multiple submissions, they must each be in a separate email.

Have a story but no way to send it electronically? You can still submit to LDP/Ca$h Presents. Send in the first three chapters, written or typed, of your completed manuscript to:

LDP: Submissions Dept
Po Box 944
Stockbridge, Ga 30281

DO NOT send original manuscript. Must be a duplicate.

Provide your synopsis and a cover letter containing your full contact information.

Thanks for considering LDP and Ca$h Presents.

Coke Kings 4

Coming Soon from Lock Down Publications/Ca$h Presents

BOW DOWN TO MY GANGSTA
By **Ca$h**
TORN BETWEEN TWO
By **Coffee**
THE STREETS STAINED MY SOUL **II**
By **Marcellus Allen**
BLOOD OF A BOSS **VI**
SHADOWS OF THE GAME II
By **Askari**
LOYAL TO THE GAME **IV**
By **T.J. & Jelissa**
A DOPEBOY'S PRAYER **II**
By **Eddie "Wolf" Lee**
IF LOVING YOU IS WRONG… **III**
By **Jelissa**
TRUE SAVAGE **VII**
MIDNIGHT CARTEL III
DOPE BOY MAGIC IV
By **Chris Green**
BLAST FOR ME **III**
A SAVAGE DOPEBOY III
CUTTHROAT MAFIA II
By **Ghost**
A HUSTLER'S DECEIT III
KILL ZONE **II**

T.J. Edwards

BAE BELONGS TO ME III
A DOPE BOY'S QUEEN II
By **Aryanna**
CHAINED TO THE STREETS III
By **J-Blunt**
COKE KINGS V
KING OF THE TRAP II
By **T.J. Edwards**
GORILLAZ IN THE BAY V
TEARS OF A GANGSTA II
De'Kari
THE STREETS ARE CALLING II
Duquie Wilson
KINGPIN KILLAZ IV
STREET KINGS III
PAID IN BLOOD III
CARTEL KILLAZ IV
DOPE GODS II
Hood Rich
SINS OF A HUSTLA II
ASAD
TRIGGADALE III
Elijah R. Freeman
KINGZ OF THE GAME V
Playa Ray
SLAUGHTER GANG IV
RUTHLESS HEART IV

Coke Kings 4

By Willie Slaughter
THE HEART OF A SAVAGE III
By Jibril Williams
FUK SHYT II
By Blakk Diamond
THE DOPEMAN'S BODYGAURD II
By Tranay Adams
TRAP GOD II
By Troublesome
YAYO III
A SHOOTER'S AMBITION III
By S. Allen
GHOST MOB
Stilloan Robinson
KINGPIN DREAMS II
By Paper Boi Rari
CREAM
By Yolanda Moore
SON OF A DOPE FIEND II
By Renta
FOREVER GANGSTA II
GLOCKS ON SATIN SHEETS II
By Adrian Dulan
LOYALTY AIN'T PROMISED II
By Keith Williams
THE PRICE YOU PAY FOR LOVE II
DOPE GIRL MAGIC II

T.J. Edwards

By Destiny Skai
TOE TAGZ III
By Ah'Million
CONFESSIONS OF A GANGSTA II
By Nicholas Lock
I'M NOTHING WITHOUT HIS LOVE II
By Monet Dragun
CAUGHT UP IN THE LIFE II
By Robert Baptiste
NEW TO THE GAME III
By **Malik D. Rice**
LIFE OF A SAVAGE III
By **Romell Tukes**
QUIET MONEY II
By **Trai'Quan**
THE STREETS MADE ME II
By **Larry D. Wright**
THE ULTIMATE SACRIFICE VI
By **Anthony Fields**
THE LIFE OF A HOOD STAR
By Ca$h & Rashia Wilson

<u>**Available Now**</u>

RESTRAINING ORDER **I & II**

Coke Kings 4

By **CA$H & Coffee**
LOVE KNOWS NO BOUNDARIES **I II & III**
By **Coffee**
RAISED AS A GOON I, II, III & IV
BRED BY THE SLUMS I, II, III
BLAST FOR ME I & II
ROTTEN TO THE CORE I II III
A BRONX TALE I, II, III
DUFFEL BAG CARTEL I II III IV
HEARTLESS GOON I II III IV
A SAVAGE DOPEBOY I II
HEARTLESS GOON I II III
DRUG LORDS I II III
CUTTHROAT MAFIA
By **Ghost**
LAY IT DOWN **I & II**
LAST OF A DYING BREED
BLOOD STAINS OF A SHOTTA I & II III
By **Jamaica**
LOYAL TO THE GAME I II III
LIFE OF SIN I, II III
By **TJ & Jelissa**
BLOODY COMMAS I & II
SKI MASK CARTEL I II & III
KING OF NEW YORK I II,III IV V
RISE TO POWER I II III
COKE KINGS I II III IV

T.J. Edwards

BORN HEARTLESS I II III IV
KING OF THE TRAP
By **T.J. Edwards**
IF LOVING HIM IS WRONG…I & II
LOVE ME EVEN WHEN IT HURTS I II III
By **Jelissa**
WHEN THE STREETS CLAP BACK I & II III
THE HEART OF A SAVAGE I II
By **Jibril Williams**
A DISTINGUISHED THUG STOLE MY HEART I II & III
LOVE SHOULDN'T HURT I II III IV
RENEGADE BOYS I II III IV
PAID IN KARMA I II III
By **Meesha**
A GANGSTER'S CODE I &, II III
A GANGSTER'S SYN I II III
THE SAVAGE LIFE I II III
CHAINED TO THE STREETS I II
By J-Blunt
PUSH IT TO THE LIMIT
By **Bre' Hayes**
BLOOD OF A BOSS **I, II, III, IV, V**
SHADOWS OF THE GAME
By **Askari**
THE STREETS BLEED MURDER **I, II & III**
THE HEART OF A GANGSTA I II& III
By **Jerry Jackson**

Coke Kings 4

CUM FOR ME I II III IV V
An **LDP Erotica Collaboration**
BRIDE OF A HUSTLA **I II & II**
THE FETTI GIRLS **I, II& III**
CORRUPTED BY A GANGSTA I, II III, IV
BLINDED BY HIS LOVE
THE PRICE YOU PAY FOR LOVE
DOPE GIRL MAGIC
By **Destiny Skai**
WHEN A GOOD GIRL GOES BAD
By **Adrienne**
THE COST OF LOYALTY I II III
By Kweli
A GANGSTER'S REVENGE **I II III & IV**
THE BOSS MAN'S DAUGHTERS I II III IV V
A SAVAGE LOVE **I & II**
BAE BELONGS TO ME I II
A HUSTLER'S DECEIT I, II, III
WHAT BAD BITCHES DO I, II, III
SOUL OF A MONSTER I II III
KILL ZONE
A DOPE BOY'S QUEEN
By **Aryanna**
A KINGPIN'S AMBITON
A KINGPIN'S AMBITION **II**
I MURDER FOR THE DOUGH
By **Ambitious**

T.J. Edwards

TRUE SAVAGE I II III IV V VI
DOPE BOY MAGIC I, II, III
MIDNIGHT CARTEL I II
By **Chris Green**
A DOPEBOY'S PRAYER
By **Eddie "Wolf" Lee**
THE KING CARTEL **I, II & III**
By **Frank Gresham**
THESE NIGGAS AIN'T LOYAL **I, II & III**
By **Nikki Tee**
GANGSTA SHYT **I II &III**
By **CATO**
THE ULTIMATE BETRAYAL
By **Phoenix**
BOSS'N UP **I , II & III**
By **Royal Nicole**
I LOVE YOU TO DEATH
By Destiny J
I RIDE FOR MY HITTA
I STILL RIDE FOR MY HITTA
By **Misty Holt**
LOVE & CHASIN' PAPER
By **Qay Crockett**
TO DIE IN VAIN
SINS OF A HUSTLA
By **ASAD**
BROOKLYN HUSTLAZ

Coke Kings 4

By **Boogsy Morina**
BROOKLYN ON LOCK I & II
By **Sonovia**
GANGSTA CITY
By **Teddy Duke**
A DRUG KING AND HIS DIAMOND I & II III
A DOPEMAN'S RICHES
HER MAN, MINE'S TOO I, II
CASH MONEY HO'S
By Nicole Goosby
TRAPHOUSE KING **I II & III**
KINGPIN KILLAZ I II III
STREET KINGS I II
PAID IN BLOOD **I II**
CARTEL KILLAZ I II III
DOPE GODS
By **Hood Rich**
LIPSTICK KILLAH **I, II, III**
CRIME OF PASSION I II & III
By **Mimi**
STEADY MOBBN' **I, II, III**
THE STREETS STAINED MY SOUL
By **Marcellus Allen**
WHO SHOT YA **I, II, III**
SON OF A DOPE FIEND
Renta
GORILLAZ IN THE BAY **I II III IV**

T.J. Edwards

TEARS OF A GANGSTA
DE'KARI
TRIGGADALE I II
Elijah R. Freeman
GOD BLESS THE TRAPPERS I, II, III
THESE SCANDALOUS STREETS I, II, III
FEAR MY GANGSTA I, II, III
THESE STREETS DON'T LOVE NOBODY I, II
BURY ME A G I, II, III, IV, V
A GANGSTA'S EMPIRE I, II, III, IV
THE DOPEMAN'S BODYGAURD
Tranay Adams
THE STREETS ARE CALLING
Duquie Wilson
MARRIED TO A BOSS… I II III
By Destiny Skai & Chris Green
KINGZ OF THE GAME I II III IV
Playa Ray
SLAUGHTER GANG I II III
RUTHLESS HEART I II III
By Willie Slaughter
FUK SHYT
By Blakk Diamond
DON'T F#CK WITH MY HEART I II
By Linnea
ADDICTED TO THE DRAMA I II III
By Jamila

Coke Kings 4

YAYO I II
A SHOOTER'S AMBITION I II
By S. Allen
TRAP GOD
By Troublesome
FOREVER GANGSTA
GLOCKS ON SATIN SHEETS
By Adrian Dulan
TOE TAGZ I II
By Ah'Million
KINGPIN DREAMS
By Paper Boi Rari
CONFESSIONS OF A GANGSTA
By Nicholas Lock
I'M NOTHING WITHOUT HIS LOVE
By Monet Dragun
CAUGHT UP IN THE LIFE
By Robert Baptiste
NEW TO THE GAME I II
By Malik D. Rice
Life of a Savage I II
By Romell Tukes
LOYALTY AIN'T PROMISED
By Keith Williams
Quiet Money
By **Trai'Quan**
THE STREETS MADE ME

T.J. Edwards

By **Larry D. Wright**
THE ULTIMATE SACRIFICE I, II, III, IV, V
KHADIFI
By **Anthony Fields**
THE LIFE OF A HOOD STAR
By **Ca$h & Rashia Wilson**

BOOKS BY LDP'S CEO, CA$H

TRUST IN NO MAN
TRUST IN NO MAN 2
TRUST IN NO MAN 3
BONDED BY BLOOD
SHORTY GOT A THUG
THUGS CRY
THUGS CRY 2
THUGS CRY 3
TRUST NO BITCH
TRUST NO BITCH 2
TRUST NO BITCH 3
TIL MY CASKET DROPS
RESTRAINING ORDER
RESTRAINING ORDER 2
IN LOVE WITH A CONVICT
LIFE OF A HOOD STAR

Coming Soon
BONDED BY BLOOD 2
BOW DOWN TO MY GANGSTA

T.J. Edwards

Made in the USA
Columbia, SC
23 October 2021